CREEPERS2

JESSE HAYNES

CREEPERS 2
MAN'S WORST ENEMY

To Thaddeus,

Reading is MAN'S BEST FRIEND!

[signature]

TATE PUBLISHING
AND ENTERPRISES, LLC

Creepers 2
Copyright © 2016 by Jesse Haynes. All rights reserved.

No part of this publication may be reproduced, stored in a retrieval system or transmitted in any way by any means, electronic, mechanical, photocopy, recording or otherwise without the prior permission of the author except as provided by USA copyright law.

This novel is a work of fiction. Names, descriptions, entities, and incidents included in the story are products of the author's imagination. Any resemblance to actual persons, events, and entities is entirely coincidental.

The opinions expressed by the author are not necessarily those of Tate Publishing, LLC.

Published by Tate Publishing & Enterprises, LLC
127 E. Trade Center Terrace | Mustang, Oklahoma 73064 USA
1.888.361.9473 | www.tatepublishing.com

Tate Publishing is committed to excellence in the publishing industry. The company reflects the philosophy established by the founders, based on Psalm 68:11,
"The Lord gave the word and great was the company of those who published it."

Book design copyright © 2016 by Tate Publishing, LLC. All rights reserved.
Cover design by Joshua Rafols
Interior design by Richell Balansag

Published in the United States of America

ISBN: 978-1-68270-232-1
Fiction / Science Fiction / Apocalyptic & Post-Apocalyptic
16.01.27

To my loving parents,
who believed in a little boy with a dream
long before anybody else did.

1

The air was thick and heavy. The midday sun beat down on the sand of the beach, only to have the bright light reflected back while the heat was absorbed, transforming the tiny granules of sand into scorching hot coals. Waves from the ocean lapped at the sandy beach, depositing pieces of driftwood and other floating wastes on the shore and leaving them there until someone cleaned them up. It never happened, though. People were gone.

Adjacent to the beach was the large abandoned shell of a metropolis. Skyscrapers and other various complexes stretched across the skyline, but they had lost most of their resounding brilliance. The lower level windows had been sealed off with makeshift metal bars and sheets. The streets that stretched throughout this city were now littered with abandoned vehicles, which sat rusting away in the humid and hot air. The streetlights now leaned in various directions, some worse than others. Moreover, some had been snapped and were nowhere in sight. A layer of filth and trash covered almost the entire city. Strong gusts of wind would pick up papers and blow them through the air until they were eventually pinned against the side of a decrepit building or street sign.

Graffiti of various colors, sizes, meanings, and images decorated the sides of the buildings. Most were depressing, showing skulls, weeping people, and an assortment of symbols that represented death. One message, made in red lettering on the side of a hospital, announced, "There is nothing doctors can do." Another showed a pistol and said, "End your life before the creepers do." A reference to a Bible verse was on the side of a chapel in white paint, but the words, "Welcome to Hell," had been sprayed over it.

This had once been a successful city. The inhabitants had referred to it as "Miami," but that name hadn't been mentioned in the city for quite some time. Just under six years ago, an extraterrestrial virus had been brought back to earth by an astronaut who had contracted this disease on a space mission. The virus had spread rapidly, tearing apart the United States, and then eventually the world. Almost all humanity had been killed after a long and violent process.

In the brief period of studying the virus, doctors had learned that it would essentially shut down ninety percent of the host's brain and keep it at a dormant state. The host only retained basic body functions, yet it was made aggressive by the virus as well. Its body was then forced to produce and excrete an uncommonly large amount of different chemicals and substances. Excessive amounts of calcium would be created and integrated into the host's bone structure, causing bones to become denser and the teeth to be elongated into fangs. The excess production of these chemicals required fueling, so the host's fat was also broken down quickly, which would only lead to more agility. In effect, the virus would transform the host into a mindless, but incredibly successful, predator.

These mutant beasts had also been given a name. The term *creepers* had been coined in describing them. Nobody had been exactly sure where the term had originated, but the name had caught on, and in no time people worldwide were referring to these mutants as creepers. The monsters had essentially killed off all humanity. The virus that created them was proven to not be aerially contagious, but only contractible through direct exposure to saliva. This meant the creeper virus was typically spread through bite wounds. Coincidentally, creepers seemed to be hardwired to bite, so the virus spread across the globe like wildfire.

After the initial and seemingly exponential growth of creeper population, however, the number of the beasts slowly started to die off. Unknown at first was that the virus would slowly shut down the host's nervous system and eventually kill him or her, which was a process that typically lasted just over three years. This meant that not only humans were almost extinct by now, but creepers were losing numbers as well. Now there was only a small percentage as many creepers left as there once had been at the population's peak, so Miami was looking more and more like a ghost town than a monster-infested zoo.

The most movement in the city now was on the beach, where a medium-sized animal was curiously padding across the moist sand. This was a dog—dark-furred, average height, surprisingly well fed. It continued across the beach, leaving paw prints impressed in the sand and its nose feverishly sniffing so as to locate its next potential meal. The dog's mouth was slightly open, and a long tongue glistening with saliva lazily hung out. Seemingly with no cares in the world, the dog continued forward across the debris-laden beach. It stopped once to sniff at the skeletal remains of a large fish that had floated in from the ocean before continuing forward across the hot sand.

The dog was being watched. From a hundred yards away behind a dumpster in the shadows of an alley, a crouched figure had eyes locked onto the dog. This figure had dark matted hair, sickly pale skin, impressive muscles, sharp fangs, and bright yellow eyes. It was a creeper, watching the dog in solitude. The creeper moved out from behind the dumpster and crept closer to the beach. It stayed low to the ground in an expert predatorial position. This was not its first time to go on a hunt, and the allure of fresh meat seemed much more appealing than the canned food from grocery stores or abandoned homes that it had grown accustomed to eating.

The dog seemed to have perceived a slight disturbance in its environment. Its large ears erected and turned toward the alley. It sniffed. Still not completely convinced that everything was normal, it gingerly continued forward. It no longer was looking for a meal, but now was seeking some form of shelter instead.

CREEPERS 2

After temporarily pausing, the creeper continued forward in stealthy pursuit of its canine prize. It sniffed the air in an attempt to detect the dog's scent. The dog froze once again and leaned its head to the side, one ear standing erect. The creeper lowered itself down into the shadows again but not quickly enough. The dog had realized it was in danger. Without looking back, it took off running at a full sprint across the hot sand.

With a disapproving hiss, the creeper bolted out of the alley and onto the beach in pursuit. It took enormous strides that were both quick and powerful in the attempt to catch up to its prey. The dog's head snapped back around to locate its attacker, but it continued forward even faster. It whimpered in fear before veering to its left and heading back toward the city. The creeper was progressively getting closer, and by now the gap had been narrowed to sixty yards.

Making it all the way off of the beach, the dog ran up onto a street covered with dilapidated, weathered cars. It hurriedly sprinted around a small black coupe. The creeper in pursuit took an enormous leap and jumped over the car, pushing itself off of the car's roof and even higher into the air. It roared from above as it watched the dog continue forward.

The game of cat and mouse continued when the dog took a sharp right turn and bolted into an alley. It split a puddle and slipped somewhat before continuing into the shadows. The creeper never let up, only growing closer. The dog's sprint broke into a trot, which then diminished to nothing more than a walk as it saw what lay ahead: this alley was a dead end. A large brick wall stretched into the sky where the dog's only chance of escape had been. By now, the creeper also had slowed. It ran its tongue across its pointed fangs. Hungry yellow eyes locked onto the dog. The creeper was only feet away from what would soon be a tasty meal.

It dove forward, knocking the canine down and pinning it against the street. The dog let out a terrified and pained bark as sharp fangs dug into the meat around one of its hind legs. The bite did not last very long, though, because of a sudden interruption.

Another roar rang out from behind the creeper, who reeled around to see a second much larger creeper standing in the end of the alley. This creeper had apparently spotted the dog as well and followed in pursuit. Now both creepers stood in the alley staring intently at each other, but neither made any movement. It was against their instinct to share prey at any cost.

The large creeper began snarling and advancing while the original creeper stood its ground but lowered itself into a more attack-ready position. Now they were only a few feet apart, staring into each other's yellow eyes with hatred.

The smaller creeper was the first to attack. It lashed out a hand of sharp fingernails, but the pain-inflicting strike was evaded. The response came in the form of gnashing fangs from the second of the beasts. This attack was evaded as well. The large creeper, frustrated now, lowered its head and plowed forward, picking up the other creeper and slamming it into the brick wall. The wounded dog quickly stood and bolted past the wrestling beasts and limped into the sunlight, escaping as the two skirmished in the alley behind.

The creepers continued wrestling, completely unaware that their prey had escaped. Blows were exchanged and claws inflicted cuts as they continuously growled at each other. The battle showed no signs of letting up until the smaller creeper made its move. When the larger creeper lashed out with a fist, the other grabbed the hand and bit it fiercely. It continued clamping down with a bone-crushing grip for several seconds despite the wailing from its opponent. Finally, the bite was loosened, and the wounded creeper retreated out of the alley, leaving the first of the creepers alone in the shadows.

Once again, silence had been restored. The creeper looked around the alley and realized that the dog had escaped. It cried out in sorrow, the somber sound rang out in the midday. Choosing not to further pursue the dog, the hungry creeper slinked out of the alley in search of something else to eat.

The city of Miami still seemed dead. There was no sign of either the dog or the second creeper who had tried to steal the prey. The creeper explored down an empty street, stopping to inspect an overflowing trash can for anything edible. This was as unproductive as the dog chase. Finding nothing, it continued forward. It saw a group of five or six more creepers running together in the distance before disappearing behind a large skyscraper. Everything to this point seemed like an average day, but then some unusual things began to occur. In the distance, maybe a quarter of a mile away, a gunshot rang out. Another shot came in response, obviously from a different gun.

The sound of gunfire had not been heard in the city for a very long time. Gunshots meant people, and people had become extinct in Miami. The creeper instinctively began wandering in the direction of the sounds to investigate. Even more rounds of shots were fired, and the creeper broke into a trot. It ran into another alley that opened up onto a street, and then headed down the street to its right, which was in the direction of the continuing gunshots.

The gunshots ceased, leaving the creeper standing indecisively in the street. To its right was a tall building with a rusty exterior fire escape. The stairs climbed all the way to the building's roof, so the creeper headed to them and began winding up several flights. It paused the ascent for a brief second to listen for any more gunfire, but none came, so it continued up the rusty flights of stairs. Some of the stairs creaked under footfall and seemed very unsafe, but creepers were never afraid. They didn't even know how to be.

Finally, it reached the top of the stairs and emerged out onto the roof of the building. The view across the city was fantastic, and so much more was visible than from the ground. The creeper turned around slowly, scanning the skyline for any disturbance from which the gunfire might have come. While studying the city, it discovered an enormous surprise in the distance: half a mile away, there was a tall hotel building that was completely consumed in a blazing fire. Thick gray smoke billowed into the sky.

CREEPERS 2

Now overtaken by an animalistic curiosity, the creeper ventured back down the stairwell. The smell of smoke was now becoming very obvious. It trotted farther down the street, using the large pillar of smoke in the sky ahead as a means of navigation. The creeper wound its way around cars and leapt over a fallen street sign. Ahead there were two or three more creepers emerging from dark alleys and also traveling in the direction of the smoke.

Suddenly, more gunshots erupted from ahead. The curious creeper broke into a run toward the source of the disruption. It was growing closer to the burning building, which had to be less than two hundred yards away, coming into view at the end of the street. The creeper continued forward for thirty seconds but stopped when it noticed something that it had not seen in a very long time: six people were standing at the base of the building, and they seemed to be in a distressed state. It watched and assessed the situation.

At the base of the flaming building, the six men stood, and they were armed with assault rifles and wearing combat vests. They had their weapons raised and pointed away from the building, where four large, dark trucks were hastily parked. The creeper's animal-like brain struggled to understand what was happening and looked upon the scene in confusion. As it watched, the armed men opened fire toward the trucks, shooting out the windows and putting holes in the framework of the vehicles. Still, it didn't understand what the men were shooting at until there was another noticeable movement. Crouched behind one of the trucks was a teenaged girl who also had an assault rifle, but she did not appear to be using it. The men were targeting her for some reason, and her situation looked grim. The girl was yelling something, but the words were made undistinguishable, even for such an adaptive predator. She lowered her weapon even further as the men continued their approach.

The creeper advanced forward again, drawing nearer the gunfight. It was weaponless but instinctively determined to get in on the action. It stopped once again and watched. The men were converging toward the girl, who was completely helpless. She was simply outnumbered. They were closing, rifles raised, ready for the kill.

"Don't shoot!" The girl's scream was audible now. She dropped her rifle and raised her hands to the air. "Please."

Now one of the men replied, "We were instructed not to take any prisoners alive. That includes you, sweetheart." He paused and trained his rifle on the teenaged girl. "Kill her."

The men were about to open fire on the girl when there was a thunderous cracking sound from the burning building. One of the outside walls on an upper floor began crumbling. The shower of debris was small at first, but then an enormous section of wall fell outward and tumbled toward the ground. One of the armed men noticed the slab of building hurtling down toward the group, and he yelled out, but it was too late. The large piece of the building, still in flames, slammed down, completely crushing two of the trucks and five of the six men. A plume of dirt and ash burst into the sky, and a tremendous crunching sound thundered out over the crackling of the fire.

The girl rolled away from her hiding place, stood, and whirled around. She raised her rifle and sent several rounds of bullets slamming into the last of the guards, throwing him off his feet and killing him immediately. "It's about time I finally catch a break." She dusted the ash and soot off and looked up at the burning building, which had begun to partially crumble in on itself, mumbling something else that the creeper could not hear. She slowly walked away from the building as more debris showered down, and when she looked up, she locked eyes with the creeper that had been watching her the entire time. The girl blinked back a look of surprise and was about to say something when another large section of the building collapsed, sending a tremor shooting across the ground. She stumbled and fell down, dropping her rifle again.

As the creeper watched her, it didn't see a young teenager fighting for survival. Instead, it saw its next potential meal. It was still ravenously hungry, and it seized the opportunity to attack, sprinting forward across the abandoned street to the girl as she was standing up. Suddenly, an unexpected crackling of gunfire rang out from the roof of the building, and the surprised creeper briefly looked up to find the source. After a second, it disregarded the distraction and once again charged to the girl, but the brief pause had given her enough time to regain her rifle and become ready.

The girl, now on her feet with her rifle in hand, fired two shots.

Time seemed to slow for the attacking creeper. A bullet slammed into its stomach, which seemed to explode into a scorching inferno of pain. It roared in agony before the second bullet burrowed into its shoulder. The beast spiraled to the ground and skidded forward, blood oozing from the gunshot wounds. It felt as if its body had been torn apart. The bullet punctures burned white hot.

The creeper lay on its back on the cement. Its eyes looked into the cloudless sky, but they saw nothing. The pain was too great, too overbearing. As blood continued to flow from the wounds, the faint sound of footsteps drew nearer, but they still sounded as if they were coming through a long tunnel. The echoing footsteps came closer and then suddenly stopped. Its vision was slowly returning as the blinding pain slightly subsided, and soon it found that it was staring up into the face of the teenage girl. Somewhere deep down in its damaged brain stirred the feeling of recognition, as if it had seen this girl before.

The same look of recognition was also very apparent on the face of the girl. She looked completely awestruck and horrified while staring down at the creeper that was slowly dying at her feet. Before the creeper slipped into unconsciousness, the girl yelled out something, but still the beast at her feet only heard the words as dull echoes. "Oh my gosh…" The girl struggled to form the words, "You're Drake!" The creeper closed its eyes as it was overcome by pain.

2

TWO WEEKS EARLIER...

The feeling of cold fingers brushing his cheek woke Jason Bennett up. His eyes snapped open, and for a brief second he could not remember where he was or how he had arrived there. Then the memories of where he was and how he had arrived here came flooding back, and he opened his eyes hesitantly to face the soft light of another morning.

Jason was lying on an air mattress, covered with a blanket. A large camping tent encompassed him. The cold fingers that had awoken him belonged to the teenaged girl who was lying on the air mattress against him. She was very beautiful, thoughtful, and caring, which led him to develop very strong feelings for her over the three months he had been with her in this place. Her name was Michaela.

She spoke softly. "We have to get up now. Today is the day that we finally get to leave."

Jason started to sit up and mumbled, "I really don't want to go anywhere. I'm so warm and happy." His head dropped back into the pillow.

Michaela was gently insistent. "If you don't get up, then we won't be able to finish packing. C'mon, Jason." She tugged on his arm slightly in an attempt to try to coax him off of the air mattress. "Please?"

Jason opened his eyes again and looked into the loving, rich chocolaty eyes of his girlfriend. "Give me five minutes? That is all I'm asking for."

"We need to go now so we don't miss breakfast. I'm hungry." He didn't budge. "Please? Do it for me." With that, Michaela leaned forward. Her lips met with Jason's, and they kissed for several seconds. When they reluctantly broke apart, she asked, "Now, will you please get up?"

"Fine, but just for you." Jason rolled the blanket off them and welcomed the cool morning air. By getting out of his air mattress of a bed, he was not only losing the warmth of both Michaela and his blanket, but he was also walking into the horrible and frigid reality that had become his life.

Both Jason and Michaela were in a camp, along with twenty-four other people who had taken them in. Their story started much earlier though. Jason had a brother who was named Drake, and together the two of them had battled through the apocalypse and helped each other survive. They had spent all of their life in New York City, assuming they were the only humans left, until they had met another man named Fox, who lived just outside of the city. Fox convinced the brothers they should attempt to travel to a colony of survivors in Miami, and the group of three set off across the desolate country. Fox died during the trip, though, after sacrificing himself for the brothers to escape.

The brothers refused to let Fox's death go in vain, so they had completed the journey to Miami. In Miami, things had begun to look more positive. They met Michaela there, the three became good friends, and they had discovered the settlement of survivors was very real. The three teenagers had been welcomed into the literally underground settlement with open arms, but in a horrible turn of events, the settlement was wiped out during a creeper attack, and Jason's brother had been bitten and transformed into one of the beasts. The stay in Miami had ended when Jason and Michaela were chased to the beach by an enormous group of creepers, only to be saved by a helicopter that had come from the camp in which they were staying now. They had been taken back and welcomed to the camp, which had been three months ago.

Jason put a jacket on over the white T-shirt he was wearing. He took Michaela by the hand, and together they walked out of the tent and into the cool autumn air of the camp. The simple camp was in central Georgia, built in a clearing of a piney forest. To the southern side of the camp, a highway ran east and west, but Jason had never gone that far. In the camp, there were six large supply trucks, about twenty tents, and three helicopters which were almost always in use. The supplies for the camp were stored in the large airplane that had brought the campers to Georgia.

The teenagers walked across the camp grounds to a long table at which several men, most of whom were in their late twenties or early thirties, were gathering and eating eggs and toast. One of the men, a taller man with a chiseled body, and friendly eyes, greeted them, "Good morning! Did you sleep well?" He spoke with a kind tone and sounded as if he was genuinely concerned about the teenagers' welfare.

"I slept better than usual, Holder," Jason replied. "I didn't even want to get up."

This man, James Holder, was the leader of the camp. Despite his authority, he had insisted that the teenagers should refer to him on a first-name basis, yet Jason still addressed him by his last name. Holder was the man who was responsible for saving both Jason and Michaela three months ago in Miami, and he also was, coincidentally, Fox's brother-in-law, so two members of the same family were responsible for getting the teenagers to this point. Holder was a former Marine sniper, and he had been sent to Australia on a rescue mission during the apocalypse. Since he had been out of the United States during the initial outbreak of the virus, Holder had very luckily managed to survive.

Holder, dressed in combat pants and a tight green shirt with a rifle slung over his shoulder, nodded understandingly and replied, "I didn't want to get out of bed this morning either, honestly. But we have a long trip ahead of us today, and we need to get everything loaded onto the plane." He gestured over his shoulder, and Jason's eyes followed. A hundred yards away, the medium-sized passenger airplane was parked on a cleared highway that was being used as a landing strip. This plane was their ride home, and according to the plan, all of the campers plus the two teenagers were going to take it to San Francisco, where they would stay for the night, refuel, and then fly overseas to Australia the following day.

Both Jason and Michaela helped themselves to large helpings of the breakfast foods that had been prepared by one of the campers who was operating as the cook. He was a burly man named Teddy, who had an infinite amount of both smiles and chins. Teddy's only actual jobs in the camp were cooking meals and tending to the chicken coop and gardens from which the majority of their food came, be it fresh eggs, meat, or vegetables. Despite his lack of other responsibilities, however, he always seemed to stay busy helping other people do various things, and everyone enjoyed the friendly, obese man. The Georgia camp had been established with the sole intent of finding any survivors that were left in the Americas and taking them back to the motherland from which the campers had come from—Australia. Jason and Michaela had been told that the Australians had managed to find a cure for the virus and had established a city of over five thousand survivors. The reports were that the continent was completely creeper-free, so the Australians were kind enough to spread their good fortunes with others. Temporary camps of this nature had been, in turn, established across the globe, and they all functioned the same: a supply-laden plane would fly twenty or more men to the wasteland of a country, and from there the men would gather vehicles and other various things from the apocalyptical cities and use the gathered supplies to search for survivors. This meant that the men had to find helicopters and fuel, and once they did, then they would fly the helicopters to the major cities in an attempt to locate anyone who had survived. The plan was rough, and there was no chance of finding all of the survivors, yet it was also responsible for saving Jason and Michaela's life. This time, the two teenagers, however, were the only two survivors that had been discovered.

Michaela sat down at the breakfast table beside Holder, and then Jason did the same. She asked, "So we are flying to San Francisco today?"

Holder nodded, took a long draft from his cup of coffee, and then said, "Yes, ma'am. We will stay there for the night and then head overseas the next day after a refuel."

"So you're sure the plane can make it from San Francisco to Australia?"

Holder laughed. "Well, it made it from Australia to San Francisco. It's not like we have a better choice anyway."

Jason now spoke up. "What are we going to do with all of the supplies and vehicles we've gathered? Will we just leave the three helicopters here?"

"Yes." Another drink of coffee. "That is assuming that the third chopper makes it back today." There were only two helicopters on the makeshift landing pad, the other was supposedly returning from a rescue mission in Alabama. The helicopter was scheduled to arrive three days earlier, so by now the campers were preparing to leave, assuming the worst. Holder stood.

"I better go help gather some of the final supplies. I believe the loading of the plane will start at any time."

After Holder left, a period of silence beset the breakfast table. Jason and Michaela watched some of the campers begin carrying boxes and crates, stacking them on the ground nearby the plane. All around the camp, people were bustling around and gathering items, taking down tents and clearing out the grounds entirely. There were only four women in the entire camp, all of whom were the wives of other campers, and they too were working feverishly alongside their husbands.

By this time, Jason and Michaela were finishing up their breakfast, but they were alone at the table. Everybody else had left to pack, but the packing job had been easy for the two teenagers because they had almost nothing. When the campers had left for Georgia, they had brought extra clothes and other necessities with them for any refugees they might discover, but apart from their guns, the items the campers had provided were the only belongings Jason or Michaela possessed. The camp was far less civilized than the somewhat luxurious lifestyle that the Miami settlement had, but it also was keeping them alive, so there was nothing to complain about.

Jason looked at Michaela and asked, "Are we ready to go?" She began to respond but paused, a questioning look on her face. Jason asked, "Something wrong?"

"I hear something. It's distant, but I hear it."

Jason stopped making sound and began listening as well. He heard the sound too; it was a faint whirring sound coming from a great distance.

Suddenly, there was an outburst from within the camp. A man that they called Ishmael was pointing to the sky and shouting, "There she is! There is the helicopter. She made it back!"

Holder appeared from seemingly nowhere, coming to stand beside Jason. The teenagers and their older friend stood shoulder-to-shoulder and watched the helicopter grow closer. Holder was obviously surprised—his expression didn't mask the emotion. He muttered, "I thought she was gone for good."

Jason asked, "If they are days behind schedule, what do you think caused the delay?"

Holder rubbed his chin thoughtfully. "I'll be honest. I'd about given up on America. I had decided that you two were the only survivors we were going to find. It's just been so long since the apocalypse that I assumed the rest died out." He pointed to the helicopter in the sky. "I'm trying not to get too hopeful, but I'd bet that this delay only means one thing—they found a survivor, or maybe more than one. Thank God we didn't leave them. I guess we will just have to wait and see."

The wait did not last long. As the three stood on the campground and watched, the helicopter started to land. The large metallic bird circled around the camp and began descending straight down toward the flat ground in the middle. The campers were assembling all around the area. As the spinning propellers lowered closer to earth, the typhoon of strong downward winds began picking up the dead leaves lying on the ground and blowing them into the air. Jason and Michaela both covered their eyes for protection as the helicopter landed thirty yards away. After another thirty seconds, the winds died down, and they looked toward the chopper.

For a moment, nothing happened. The helicopter sat motionless in the middle of the camp apart from the rotor that was slowing slightly. After a moment, one of the doors slid open, and a man jumped to the ground. He was wearing dark combat clothing that was similar to the other soldiers in the camp. The man yelled to Holder, "We have found a survivor, but he is in critical condition. He needs immediate medical attention. I have been doing everything possible to keep him alive."

Holder nodded but remained calm. "Get the survivor out of the helicopter, and we will get to work on him."

"Yes, sir." The man turned back toward the helicopter. At this time, the pilot, who appeared to be the only other camper on the mission, pushed a gurney from the back of the long helicopter. The first man grabbed one end of the gurney, and together they lowered it to the ground and began rolling it toward Holder.

As the gurney neared, Jason was amazed at what he saw. There was a man on it, tied down with rope that wound around his wrists, ankles, and two long pieces around his waist. The man must have been in his sixties, and he had an enormous gray beard that obviously hadn't been shaved, or even combed, for several years. Leaves and sticks were grossly entangled in it. This man was conscious and obviously very displeased with his current situation. He was shaking violently and muttering beneath his breath, but the distance was too great to comprehend what he was saying.

Finally, the gurney was close enough to see the man more clearly. He had a wrinkled face and wild eyes that were open too wide, revealing distrustful pupils that darted around from place to place. The stream of words that continued to pour out of the man's mouth became clear now. "I won't let them take me. They can't. The creepers can't win. What is that smell? Smoke? Am I on fire? My dreams!"

The man was obviously not in his right mind. He kept muttering and twitching violently, struggling against the bonds of the rope. Finally, the gurney was pushed in front of Holder and left there. Jason studied the man even more closely. His rib cage was obviously protruding through his shirt, and his skin was tight and looked yellowish.

Holder now took charge after assessing the situation. "This man is dehydrated and very malnourished. This seems to have put him into a state of deliria. We have got to get him some water and food."

The man's twitching was slowing, and he suddenly stopped muttering. His eyes came into focus, and he looked up at Holder. "Please…" The words struggled to form on his lips. "Help me." He pulled against the ropes bounding him to the gurney. "Untie me…please." He closed his eyes and dropped his head back into the gurney, lying there motionless.

More and more campers were gathering around the man on the gurney. Jason and Michaela, however, were both stepping away in disbelief. It now was clear what years of solitude after the apocalypse could do psychologically, and both of the teenagers were feeling blessed that the same gripping fate hadn't beset them.

CREEPERS 2

Michaela spoke. "I can't believe what happened to this man. Jason, what if that had happened to me after my parents died?"

Jason only shook his head. "Thank God that it didn't. Living on his own with the creepers must have driven the man insane."

They both looked back toward the survivor, who was lying limp on the gurney. Holder and another camper named Beil were untying the man, and once they had removed all of the rope, Beil scooped him up and slung him over his shoulder.

Holder yelled into the crowd of campers, "Has the medical tent been packed up yet?" From somewhere in the swarm, it was announced that the medical tent was still functional. "Good," Holder continued. "Beil and I are going to take this man to the tent. Bring water, lots of water. He is seriously dehydrated."

Beil and Holder set off with the man, while the other campers began moving around in confused disarray. Jason and Michaela, knowing not what else to do, followed Holder and Beil. Things were beginning to settle down a bit when the unexpected happened: the man, who had been lying limply over Biel's shoulder, suddenly lashed out. He threw his elbow into the back of Biel's skull, which instantly sent him to his knees. Jason and Michaela gasped, watching the insane old man attack Holder. Holder was kicked in the chest, and the force of the blow was strong enough to throw him to the ground.

A wild look had spread across the crazed man's face. He bolted away in a sprint, screaming as he went. "You will never take me! I can't let the creepers have me." He veered toward his right, running around a tent and heading toward the woods.

Holder was now back on his feet. He exclaimed, "Catch that man! He needs medical attention, and I know we can help him."

Jason and Michaela followed in pursuit, reacting far more quickly than anyone else on the scene. Everyone else was standing and watching with a surprised expression and a rigid frame. Together they tailed the man, weaving around tents and piles of supplies that were being loaded onto the plane. The chase continued for several seconds, but it soon became apparent that they were closing in on the old man, who continued to whoop and yell illogical things.

They were only yards away when the man yelled out, "My house!" He enthusiastically ran toward one of the tents that had yet to be taken down. He dove inside and disappeared from sight. An eerie feeling of unknowing settled over the campground. The teenagers slowed to a walk and began cautiously approaching the tent while trying to see what was inside.

Jason opened his mouth as if he were going to speak and then closed it indecisively. He paused for a moment, considering the situation, and then called out, "Um, sir? We can help you! Just come out, and we will cure you!"

The deranged response came in a too high-pitched of a voice for an elderly man. First, there was a wild cackle and then, "You think you can help me? You all are creepers! I won't let you have me!"

Other campers were now rushing up to surround the tent. Michaela tried her luck now. "You don't understand. We aren't creepers!" She paused, but no response came. "My boyfriend and I know how you feel…I think. We survived the apocalypse too. Come out, and we can fix you!"

The rest of the campers were completely surrounding the tent now, waiting in anticipation for the man's response. Finally, it came. "I will come out." There was a mass sigh from all of the campers together. They watched as the old man began to slowly emerge out of the tent. His head appeared first, and then his tattered clothing, and then his arms.

And then the gun.

Clutched in the man's right hand was a shiny nine millimeter pistol that he waved around at all of the campers. His eyes were spread wide, and his gun-bearing hand was twitching violently. He looked around at his startled audience and then began muttering, "There are too many of them! The creepers have taken me! It's over." The man looked defeated, and he lowered the pistol to his side.

Holder, who was standing tensely by Jason, mumbled, "Thank God." He began cautiously approaching the crazed man, and the rest of the campers watched entranced as the scene unfolded before them. Holder said, "Don't worry, sir. We aren't creepers. We all survived the apocalypse, and we have a cure."

"No!" The man once again started yelling, clutching the pistol tightly. "No more lies! I won't let you creepers take me. I can't."

Then he made his move. The campers froze, watching in disbelief. Holder was closing in and reaching out his hand to grab the man. In a flash, the man jumped back and yelled, "No! You can't do that!" He raised the pistol and aimed. Holder jumped, but he was too late. The man pulled the trigger, and a gunshot rang out in the early morning.

3

Jason and Michaela sat down on the airplane in side-by-side seats, but neither of them spoke. The entire cabin was silent, and a tragic feeling hung in the air above the campers. In each of their heads, the mental image kept playing over and over again. The gunshot. The scream. The blood. It had been a terrible experience in the entirety, and Jason wished he hadn't seen any of it.

Michaela grabbed Jason's hand and held it tightly. She too was thinking about what she'd seen. Images kept reoccurring in her brain despite her trying to push them back. She remembered the insane man raising his pistol and holding it to his head. Holder had tried to jump at the man and wrestle the gun away, but his efforts came too late. The man had pulled the trigger, and the bullet had torn a hole through the side of his skull. A shower of blood spatter and obliterated brain tissue had been thrown on Holder as he caught the man's dead body, but his effort to save the man had come too late.

In the three hours that passed since they had all witnessed the horrible suicide, the campers finished loading the airplane while Holder bathed in a nearby creek. Finally, after everything was packed, the vehicles had been tended to. Both the helicopters and the six trucks were cleaned out, parked, and refueled so if the Australians ever returned to this campsite, they would instantly have transportation.

Jason and Michaela looked out the window by their seats, scanning the camp one last time from inside the plane. They saw the fire pit, the vehicles, the creek, and in the middle of all of it was a freshly dug grave. A smooth rock stood at the head of the grave, and a permanent marker had been used to inscribe on it the words, "For all of the Americans lost to the virus."

Jason's mind was deep at work. He was thinking about the headstone, the permanent marker epitaph, and what everything meant. After five months of searching the largest cities in America, he and his girlfriend were the only two survivors found in their right minds. The rest of the entire United States population was being honored on a tombstone of a mysterious man who'd gone completely insane. The scariest thing to Jason, however, was that the crazed man was probably a good symbol to represent the American population in its final days. He remembered how out of control everybody had gone. Drugs, sex, and gangs had contested creepers for their spot on the streets of New York City at higher amounts than ever before. There had been murders, even sometimes brother against brother. Humanity had turned savage, and human survival instinct had taken over.

The sound of Holder's voice snapped Jason out of his meditative state. "All right, ladies and gentlemen," he called out as he became the last one to board the plane. "Everything here is packed up and ready to go. We will be departing momentarily." With that, he walked purposefully down the aisle of the passenger plane before sitting down in the seat directly in front of Jason. He turned around and smiled at the teenagers. "Next stop, San Francisco, California."

From somewhere over their heads, a loudspeaker crackled to life. "Please take your seats, as the plane will begin its takeoff in just a minute." Everyone was already sitting down. There was a brief moment of anticipation, and then came a tremendous lurch as the plane began to roll forward slightly. It moved slowly at first but eventually began gaining speed.

"I've never flown in a plane before," Michaela admitted.

"I have flown in a helicopter some. Of course, there was when we flew from Miami to Georgia. And I flew in a helicopter with my father a lot because he was a helicopter pilot. But that was way back when I was five or six years old, so I don't remember much at all," Jason replied.

The large plane began gaining more and more speed as it rolled down the makeshift runway. In the distance, trees were whizzing by at dizzying speeds, so Jason took his eye from the window. He looked at Michaela instead, and they smiled at each other halfheartedly. Jason knew that with every passing second, he was growing further and further away from his brother, who had been transformed into a creeper at Miami, and he couldn't help but wonder if he would ever see Drake again. He forced the thoughts back and worried about what was at hand—survival. The ground was growing more distant now, so he leaned back in his seat and closed his eyes in an attempt to fall asleep.

Jason couldn't manage to get the image of the man killing himself out of his head, so he reluctantly gave up his feeble attempt at resting. He felt Michaela lean her head against his shoulder as the plane rose higher in the sky. They sat that way for over half an hour. The cabin stayed awkwardly silent since everybody seemed afraid to talk, but after a while, the campers began to forget about what had happened and started talking among themselves. Jason sat wide awake and listened to the chatter of various conversations from throughout the cabin, but Michaela managed to fall asleep leaning against him.

He began thinking of how badly he missed his brother. He remembered watching the creeper that had once been Drake Bennett disappear into the abandoned city of Miami as he and Michaela were escaping in a helicopter with Holder. There had been so many unanswered questions at that time, and he still did not have an answer to some of them. He wasn't sure what his future held, but he knew that somehow he had to get back to the United States with the cure so that he could attempt to save his brother. The virus was slowly killing Drake with every day that passed, so time was the true enemy.

The deep thinking was once again interrupted by the voice of Holder, who asked, "So are you excited to finally get to see Australia? You've been stuck in our camp for a very long time now."

Jason paused for a moment, trying to escape his trance and process what had just been said to him. He collected his thoughts and responded, "Yeah, I'm finally going to have a safe place to call home again."

Holder smiled understandingly. "I think you will probably like the colony. I know for a fact that there will be a lot of respect for you and your girlfriend. After all, you are the only survivors we found from the United States. You two and me, that is."

Jason knew that Holder had once been a Marine from America who had happened to be in Australia when the viral outbreak had occurred, but still he had not considered Holder as "American." The thought made him feel closer to Holder, as if they were more closely related. He asked, "So where will we live in the colony? Will we have our own tent?"

At this, Holder chuckled before responding, "I promise that our colony is far more civilized than the camp was. There are houses and living quarters, and I suspect you will be pleased with where you stay." There was a look of certainty in his eyes.

Jason jokingly pressed. "What is that supposed to mean?"

Shaking his head, Holder replied, "I'll just leave that as a surprise to you. All I'm going to say is that you will be happy where you are staying."

"Do you have electricity?"

Completely ignoring the question, Holder asked, "Did I ever tell you about how the colony was founded? It's a very interesting story."

Jason shook his head. "I don't think I've ever gotten the complete story, just bits and pieces from conversations with you."

Holder nodded and pointed out the window at an abandoned city. "Seeing cities like this just makes me shake my head. It is absolutely mind-boggling that something as simple as a virus can take out an entire nation."

Jason studied the city visible far below them and couldn't even guess what city he was looking at. They all looked the same: tall buildings, trash, streets full of abandoned cars, graffiti, and no humans in sight. The deadly stillness was something he had never gotten used to, no matter how much time had passed since the apocalypse.

Holder continued after the brief distraction. "I was in Australia on the rescue mission when we first got word of the plague. It took us all by surprise, really. And by 'us,' I mean the group of three other men who were with me on the mission." He paused in recollection. "We knew that the United States military was going to need our help controlling the panic in the streets, so we decided to abort the mission and return to the United States."

Thinking back to his conversations with Fox, Holder's brother-in-law, Jason questioned, "Fox said that you never came home from Australia after the apocalypse. Did he not know that you returned?"

Holder shook his head again. "No, Fox was right. After more thinking, my group decided that we couldn't completely abort the mission, so we drew straws to see who would stay in Australia and remain there as a spy until the other help could return. I got the short straw." His voice was monotone, but Jason could still tell this was a subject his friend struggled to discuss.

"I'm really sorry."

"The plans were made, and I was going to stay as a spy. I called my wife, who was pregnant at the time, and asked her to come to Australia with me, but she said she knew that I wouldn't be gone long. She also said that she knew the baby was close, so she didn't want to make the trip, so I promised her I wouldn't be gone for more than two months." He blinked back what might have been a tear.

Jason didn't know what to say. He felt terrible for Holder, but couldn't figure out how to comfort the grown military man. "I'm really sorry." He lamely apologized.

Holder forced a smile. "I'm sure you know that the virus spread across the United States in less than two months, so I never saw my wife again, and my son was never born. I'll be honest, I was suicidal, but I knew that killing myself would do absolutely no good. I decided that I would use my anger for good, and I swore to myself that I wouldn't stop until the virus had been cured. I still struggle killing creepers, knowing that any one of them could've been my wife, and I'm sure that you feel the same way about your brother."

Jason nodded and admitted. "In Miami, I realized that the creepers aren't my enemy. They are just sick people that need a cure, and I want to help cure them. I need my brother back."

"And that's exactly what we are going to do—get Drake back. I know my wife is gone by this point, but there is still hope that you can save Drake. Now let me get back to the story." His voice had become more strong and determined now. "I stayed in Australia, but people fleeing the United States brought the virus with them. Australia was better prepared for the onslaught of death and creepers, however. The city I was living in at the time established a quarantine to keep anyone and anything else out. It might have been a selfish move, but it was the logical choice. Since the virus isn't spread aerially, we kept the plague out."

Jason was beginning to think the Australians didn't sound as nearly as heroic as they did at first. He asked, "So they just set up a quarantine and left everyone else outside to go through hell?"

As if realizing just how bad the scenario sounded, Holder backtracked and clarified. "No, after the initial quarantine was set up, we built up an underground tunnel system that would allow people into the quarantine, assuming they passed a medical exam with one of our doctors to prove they were uninfected."

"Oh, that sounds much better. So when was the cure invented?"

"Yeah, let me get back to that." Holder continued the recollection. "The society was beginning to flourish after about six months. We had a team of many brilliant medical minds that were working to find a cure, and the team was led by one of my good friends named Thomas Shade. It was about that same time when the men who had helped set up the colony, me included, decided we needed a form of government. By that time, most of Australia was dead and gone."

"Did you write your own constitution?" Jason was imagining this Australian colony like the original thirteen colonies in America in some ways.

"No, it was nothing to that extent. There was a group of about twenty of us, and we appointed a man as the leader. His name is Jeffery Gordon. Gordon's not an Australian prime minister, nor is he an American president, but he might be somewhere in between. He has the ability to call the shots, but we established the board of trustees that must approve all of the major decisions. I am on the board."

Jason questioned, "How many men are on it?"

"Fourteen. All of them are from different groups too. For example, I've been named head of Australian security and the rescue missions because of my prior military training and experience." Jason was surprised at this statement. He never knew how important Holder actually was in the Australian society. "Anyway, Gordon used his power and leadership to organize a strategic medical approach for beating the virus. He had me lead a small force that went to surrounding cities to gather medical supplies and equipment for the team of eight doctors we had in the quarantine."

The sudden arousing of Michaela put the conversation on hold. She sat up and looked between Jason and Holder. "Are we almost to California?"

"Not quite."

At this, she closed her eyes and laid her head back down on Jason's shoulder. Jason chuckled and told Holder to continue the story.

By now, most of the campers had fallen asleep, and the cabin was considerably quieter. "After about three months, the cure was invented. It was tested on several subjects, and all the tests came back to support we had found a cure for the virus."

Jason asked, "Do you know how the cure works?"

Holder shook his head. "I have no idea. I just do what the doctors tell me. All I know is that right now the cure is a vaccine in a syringe, and it only works if the host allows it to be injected, so to cure a creeper, it pretty much has to be sedated. That's what makes administering the cure difficult. On the bright side, when we left for this mission, Shade and the doctors were trying to devise a way to cure creepers on a larger scale, so we will just have to see what they found."

That idea excited Jason. "Oh, I hope they managed to figure it out! Wouldn't it be fantastic if we could cure several creepers at once?"

"It would." Holder nodded. "But there has been no way to contact the Australia colony for five months, so we just don't know what they discovered."

"What will we do when we first get to Australia? Find a place to stay?"

Holder's answer surprised Jason. He said, "Well, first, I imagine they will vaccinate you against the virus." The look on Jason's face obviously showed his amazement because Holder asked, "Did you not figure we had an inoculation?"

The thought made sense to Jason, but he had not ever considered it. It was obvious that a vaccine could exist because a cure had been found, but the idea of mass immunity to the virus was almost unfathomable. The virus had been so much more volatile and destructive than any other sickness before that Jason had never thought about being inoculated against it. It had seemed like a super-virus, but the inoculation slightly took the edge from the terror associated with it.

He had heard enough that he knew he needed time to think about everything that he had been told, so he said, "Everything sounds so amazing, but I think I'm going to try to rest for a bit if you don't mind, Holder."

Holder gave Jason a kind smile in return and said, "That is not a problem. I know I've told you a lot, but don't worry about Australia. Things there are going to be relaxed, and you will be accepted into the society with open arms. I can assure you that."

"Well, thanks for all of the information you gave me," Jason answered. "I'm very excited to get to Australia." Holder turned around, so Jason laid back into his seat, keeping his arm wrapped around Michaela.

This time, falling asleep took no time at all. He slipped into a deep dreamless sleep that lasted for several hours. When he finally awoke, the plane was flying above California, and within the next thirty minutes, it was landing on the ground in San Francisco. That evening, as they pitched a tent for the night, Jason recounted to Michaela everything that Holder had told him about Australia. As night fell, the Georgia camp was distant in both of the teenagers' minds, for they were looking ahead to the future. After another hour, both of them were asleep in their tent, dreaming of the opportunities that they would surely discover overseas the following day.

Meanwhile, as the teenagers slept, other campers were finishing up the work that needed to be done. Holder and a group of four other men refueled the plane so that it would be ready for the direct flight to Australia, while others ran maintenance checks on the plane to make sure it was physically capable of the long trip. By ten o'clock that night, all of the campers were asleep apart from the shifts that were alternating through night watch patrol. Everyone was happy, knowing that they would soon be returning to their homes, friends, and family the next day.

4

The dense foliage broke up the harsh sunlight that was shining down from directly above. The forest was a mixture of bright patches and dark shadows. Two people silently prowled through the thick forest, rifles clutched in their grasps. In a clearing less than seventy yards ahead of them, a buck deer was grazing, head down, and seemingly oblivious to the world around it. This was their prey. This deer could be their food for up to a month if they could make the kill. The older of the two, a woman in her mid-thirties, whispered, "Anna, if you move a couple yards to your right, will you be able to get a clear shot around that tree?"

The second person, a sixteen-year-old girl, nodded and whispered back, "I believe so. Let me check." She took three silent steps away from the woman and dropped to one knee, positioning her rifle so that she was ready to take a shot. "Clear," she said.

"All right, good. We will shoot on three."

"One…"

"Two…"

As both of the ladies' fingers tightened on the trigger, the deer jumped and began sprinting away. Anna swore and said, "I guess we spooked it, Tanya."

Tanya, the older of the two, shook her head. "There is no way it heard us from here. We were way too quiet."

"Look!" Anna pointed back to the deer, and their question was immediately answered. Fifty feet behind it, two creepers burst into sight from within the thick woods. They were snarling, hissing, and shrieking at the deer, which fearfully snorted as it sprinted away.

"It looks like they had the same dinner plans as us," Tanya said. "Stay alert."

As they watched, the two creepers quickly closed in on the deer. The creeper that was leading the charge leapt in the air, diving at its prey.

Anna could not help herself, not wanting to watch the deer get mutilated by the vicious beasts. "No!" She yelled out at the creepers as she took aim with her rifle before unleashing a bullet that whizzed across the woodlands, tearing through the underbrush and slamming into the shoulder of one of the creepers. The creeper bellowed out in pain as the terrified deer sprinted away.

Both beasts then turned to face Anna and Tanya.

"Looks like they found us," Tanya said. "Hurry and reload."

"I'm trying," Anna replied as she stood up.

The creepers suddenly began sprinting forward, coming right at the two hunters. One was bleeding profusely from the wound in its shoulder, but that did not slow it down at all. Tanya was waving her gun around and then yelled out, "I can't get a clear shot for all of these trees."

Anna gritted her teeth, admitting, "Me either." She swore again. "They are closing in."

"Run!" As soon as she yelled the single word out, Tanya turned around and bolted into the forest. Anna followed in close pursuit, weaving through the forest thicket to the best of her ability, but still their top speed was no match for that of the creepers.

The two ran as fast as they possibly could, but frequent glances over their shoulders revealed that the predators were only gaining more ground. They were only twenty feet away when the forest broke way to an enormous clearing.

As they continued forward at a full sprint, Tanya one-handedly slung her rifle behind her and took aim. Praying for a stroke of luck, she pulled the trigger, and the creeper leading the charge dropped immediately as the bullet pierced its chest.

"Nice shot," Anna called out.

Still the other creeper was closing in on them. It was the one that was bleeding, and the wound seemed to make it even angrier. It was so close that Anna could hear its snarls right behind her. She knew that if she did not make her move soon, then the beast would pounce on her.

She slammed her heels into the ground, stopping in her tracks. The creeper continued barreling forward, and as it neared, Anna took her rifle by the barrel and swung it around with all of her strength.

For just a moment, there was a look of fear in the eyes of the beast. Then a sickening crunch rang out as the butt of her rifle struck the creeper in the skull, fracturing it completely and unleashing a flow of blood. It dropped dead instantly at her feet.

Both ladies stooped over, panting, hands on knees. The freshly dead creepers were undergoing muscle spasms on the ground nearby. Finally, Tanya managed to chuckle and say, "You just had to save that deer from them, didn't you?"

After taking a deep breath, Anna answered, "I didn't want the creepers to kill it, so I had to do something!"

"But we were just about to kill it though, so there is not much of a difference." Tanya argued.

Anna thought for a moment and then said, "Would you rather be shot and killed instantly or torn apart by a pack of creepers?"

There was a brief pause then. "You're completely right. I understand."

Anna stood straight up and began looking around her. She had been living with Tanya here in this forest for about five years now, but had never been to this clearing before. This was uncharted territory. Finally, for the first time since she could remember, this day was not routine. It was not the same hunting trip, going along the same path, looking for the same animals to make the same meals so that they could do the same thing the next day. Finally, something had changed.

Even though their lives had become very standard, their story was unique. When the virus had struck, Tanya, who was a new mother at the time, fled from the east coast to her grandparents' land in southeastern Oklahoma, believing that being in an isolated woodland area would give her the best odds of survival. She had met Anna in Alabama—an eleven-year-old orphan who had run away from her foster home to try to survive the virus as it spread. The two instantly bonded, and Anna had been living with Tanya and her five-year-old son ever since. Tanya's husband had been killed by the virus, so Anna and her son were the only family she had left. None of them lost hope, though, believing that there were other survivors out there with a story similar to theirs.

Anna turned slowly, scanning the clearing, until she froze in place. "What on earth…" She pointed to a very large metallic object imbedded into the ground some fifty yards away.

Tanya turned to see the same thing, and she gasped out, "That is an airplane!"

She was right. Upon closer examination, Anna identified the foreign object to be the remnants of a wrecked airplane complete with a jagged scar in the ground that trailed behind the plane for a considerable distance. She began jogging to the crash site, Tanya at her heels. They advanced in silence until they were finally upon the wreckage.

They examined it in silence. The plane was large enough that Anna estimated the wingspan, if the wings were still attached, to be around eighty feet. Instead, pieces of the wings had been left behind in the clearing. A hole had been torn in the side of the plane, and a look inside revealed no corpses. Anna asked, "Where are the bodies?"

Tanya's response came. "This is a drone. A very big drone. There are no bodies, and a drone doesn't have pilots or passengers. I saw several of these in my days with the military." She advanced forward once again, ducking down and disappearing into the hole in the side of the plane. "C'mon, let's see what is inside."

Anna followed her into the ghostly plane, examining the contents of the main body of storage inside, which was full of gears, levers, conveyer belts, and crates. "What is all of this stuff for?"

Tanya bit her lip, contemplating. She finally answered, "I think that this was once a medical drone, which was designed to drop medical supplies. These things were just coming out when the virus struck." She walked over to one of the crates inside and looked at it. "But I think that it was reworked to drop these crates."

The curiosity of what was inside instantly overwhelmed Anna so she asked, "Can we open one? A crate, I mean."

"Sure," Tanya answered with a nod. "Give me a hand though." She grabbed the lid of the crate and began prying on it. Anna joined in, and after a struggle, the lid came off and clattered to the metallic floor below them.

"Wow..." Together they gasped as they looked at what was inside. On the top was packaged and canned food, and as they rummaged deeper into the crate, they found weapons and ammunition and then medical supplies.

"This is the perfect collection of survival supplies," Tanya said, taking an AK-47 from the crate. "This would have been useful to have a while ago." Tanya found a cinch bag and began packing it full of groceries, and even weapons such as knives and ammunition.

"Look at this!" Anna had picked up the crate, and she showed the inside of the lid to Tanya. Printed inside the lids were words that would forever change their lives: PACKAGED IN MIAMI, FLORIDA. DECEMBER 2021.

"I don't believe it." This was the only response from Tanya for nearly a minute until finally she added, "That was only about six months ago. That can only mean one thing…"

"There are people out there. People in Miami." Anna filled in the blank for her and then asked, "So what does this mean?"

Tanya had already turned and began climbing out of the plane and back into the bright midday light with the AK-47 still in hand. "This means that we are going to Miami."

After almost half an hour of retracing their steps, winding back through the forest, and searching for their normal path, finally Tanya and Anna recognized some landmarks from their normal hunting route, which they followed back as they had come until they reached the house that they were living in: a small brick home that had formerly belonged to Tanya's grandparents, who had both died about three years before the virus had struck. The house had no electricity and no running water, but still it was better than nothing, and it was the place they had called home for quite some time.

Outside of the house was parked Tanya's car, which had sat in the same place for the past five years, apart from the biannual five-mile trip she would take just to make sure the car stayed in working condition. Beside the car was a large stockpile of fuel tanks that she had the foresight to gather before settling at the house during the virus years, hoping that one day they would be usable in making a trip like the one that seemed to be looming in their near future.

Tanya knocked on the door of the house and called out, "It is just us." She turned the doorknob and opened the door, stepping into the house. Anna followed close behind.

On the couch in the house's living room sat a five-year-old boy with sandy blond hair like his mother's, a smile that was missing a front tooth, and sea-blue eyes. He looked up from a magazine as Tanya and Anna entered the house, greeting, "I guess you didn't shoot anything, Mom?"

"Not this time."

"Did you see anything?"

"We did, but then two creepers showed up and chased it away. They chased us too." This came from Anna, who made sure that the safety was active on her rifle as she leaned it against the wall.

Tanya, who was also setting down her rifle and her new AK-47, added, "We killed them, though, JR."

"Good," JR said. "It has been a while since you saw any creepers."

Anna walked to a large piece of paper hanging on the wall that had been made into a calendar. She studied it and said, "We haven't seen a creeper for thirty-two days before today."

"Yeah, it's beginning to happen less and less." Tanya sat down on the couch beside her son and said, "But we do have some exciting news, JR. I think you are really going to like this."

The boy sounded inquisitive, asking, "What is it?"

With that, both Tanya and Anna began to explain how they had found the crashed drone, what had been inside, and the significance of the discovery. By the end of the story, JR was so excited that he was fidgeting in his seat. When they were finally done talking, he asked, "Does this mean that we are going to Miami?"

"It does, sweetie," Tanya said as she tousled her son's hair.

JR looked up to Anna, who was pretty much a sister to him. "Are you excited?" He asked the question as he looked up into her eyes before adding, "I have always wanted to meet other people. I think that would be so fun!" He then stood up from the couch and said, "I will go get my stuff together."

His mother objected. "Not so fast, young man. We still have to do your daily reading lesson before we go." She pointed to a stack of gardening magazines that she had been using to teach her son how to read.

"But, Mom!" His shoulders sagged dejectedly. "One day won't hurt anything."

Tanya laughed. "All right, sweetie, I guess you are right, especially since we did your math this morning.

Go get to packing, and Anna and I will do the same. We are going to drive my car, and I believe we can make it all the way to Miami with my stockpile of fuel."

"Are we leaving tomorrow?"

Tanya shook her head. "It's been five years. I don't think waiting a little longer will hurt anything. Plus, we have to be prepared before we leave. I'll cook up food and stuff for the trip just in case it takes longer than we expect."

Seemingly content with the answer, JR began roaming down the windowless hallway, disappearing into the shadows. Tanya was just standing from the couch when the completely unexpected happened: the quiet and hopeful mood inside the house was shattered when the front door exploded off its hinges.

"What the..."Anna began to speak, but Tanya grabbed her and shoved her across the room out of harm's immediate way.

Both women turned at the same time to see a creeper dive into the house in a flash of fangs and yellow eyes. The beast snarled violently and locked eyes with Tanya, whose weapons were next to Anna's on the complete opposite side of the room. She swore. In the distance, she heard her son scream in terror, so she yelled out, "Shut yourself in your room, JR."

"It must have heard us in the woods earlier and managed to track us back here." Anna reasoned, taking two slow steps backward. The creeper continued to growl at her and her friend, sizing them up from afar.

Tanya cast glances around the room, trying to locate anything that could be used as a weapon against the creeper, but there was no obvious choice. They were being backed into the dining room, which was a barren room apart from a table and three chairs. "Stay back, Anna," she warned through gritted teeth. "If anything happens to me, take JR and go to Miami."

Anna did not immediately respond, eyeing the creeper as it slowly advanced. She eventually said, "Remember that time when you said you wanted to teach me to drive? This probably isn't the best time to point this out, but we never got around to that."

"Oh, yes. Lovely." Tanya couldn't keep from chuckling lightly. She reached back behind her, brushing her fingers against one of the wooden chairs and then grabbing onto it tightly.

Her timing couldn't have been better. The monster dove forward almost immediately as she gripped the chair, which she pulled in front of her and used the legs to jab at the creeper, striking it in the chest. There was another flash of fangs, and the creeper bit one of the chair legs completely off. "Are you kidding me?" Tanya spat the phrase as the chair's leg dropped to the floor.

While Tanya was keeping the beast at bay, Anna turned to the window. She ran her eyes up and down it, coming up with an idea. In one swift motion, she tore the drapery down from the window while yelling, "Head's up, Tanya." The teenaged girl threw the window drapes toward the creeper, and they covered it, completely blocking its vision.

While the creeper fought at the drapes, Anna ran across the room, grabbing the new assault rifle and aiming it to get a clear shot. Tanya weaved back and forth in the dining room, attempting to stay out of the creeper's way. Finally, she lunged forward with the chair again, striking the blinded beast and knocking it into the living room and yelling, "Now!"

Anna unleashed a spray of bullets, which peppered the writhing drapery. The creeper dropped almost instantly, and its blood began staining the white material a deep crimson.

"Nice shot," Tanya said. "That was a first."

"Yes, I really thought we were goners," Anna said with a long exhalation.

A third voice came from behind them, the voice of JR. "That was scary."

"Very," the women answered in unison. Tanya added, "But I think that is a sign. That is a sign that we need to get our things together and then go to Miami."

All three people smiled, and then Anna laughed and added, "But first, we are going to need a new door."

There was much to do, and they began setting to work.

5

Gravity seemed to shift as the plane began to finally decrease in altitude, slanting out of the dark sky and downward toward the long gray stretch of a runway that stood out on the ground below. Jason's gaze was fixated out of the window beside him. What he saw was absolutely breathtaking. While gazing out into the light of the dying day, his eyes were feasting upon a bustling city that was preparing for the approaching night.

As far as he could see, buildings and homes stretched into the skyline. From their windows illuminated the recognizable warm glow of light. He murmured one word, "Electricity." People were shuffling through the streets, carrying baskets of food, groceries, clothing, or other various objects. He spotted two children playing with a shaggy pet dog near an operating fountain. Other people were pointing into the sky at the plane and talking among themselves.

Everything to this point had gone well and as planned. Jason and Michaela had slept soundly during their last night in the United States while the plane was refueled before the rest of the campers caught up on some much-needed rest. Everybody had gotten out of bed early the next morning to a hearty breakfast prepared by Teddy, and then the final preparations had been made before the intercontinental journey had begun. The airplane had left San Francisco at ten o'clock, and now they were nearing Australia about ten hours later.

The pilot's voice crackled over the loudspeaker. "We will be landing momentarily. For your own safety, do not move about the cabin until we have come to a stop." The plane's descent became even sharper now, rapidly approaching the runway below.

Just as she had been during the trip to California, Michaela was once again asleep, leaning on Jason's shoulder. He took her hand and squeezed it. "Wake up. We are here."

Her eyes snapped open, and she immediately looked out the window. She studied the scene for a brief period and then breathed, "Oh, wow. This place is amazing." Her words described the Australian city perfectly. It looked like something that had existed before the apocalypse, a perfectly preserved time capsule that somehow buried the memories of the virus and the fall of humanity. To the teenagers, the entire city buzzed with hope.

The plane suddenly lurched as it made contact with the ground. It continued forward down the runway, slowing slightly with more distance. Jason and Michaela continued gazing out of the window as the buildings passed, now at their eye level. As opposed to all the places they had been, this city had no skyscrapers. All of the buildings appeared clean, and some of them were obviously recently constructed. They shared similar features that pointed to the architectural work being done by one or two people.

Jason had become so absorbed in studying the features of the buildings that he hadn't realized the plane had stopped until the pilot's voice announced, "It is now safe to move about the cabin. I hope you all are as glad to be back home as I am."

Jason looked at Michaela. "Well, what do we do now?"

People in the plane were beginning to chatter happily. For some, the arrival meant being reunited with family after over five months away. Others were just glad to be back home to a routine and safety. From the back of the plane came Holder's voice calling out to the teenagers. "You two can come with me. We will get off of the plane first."

Jason and Michaela stood up as Holder walked down the aisle toward them. He passed them, and they followed him out of the plane's cabin. The group of three reached the exit ramp, and Holder turned back to whisper, "Everyone will be gathering around. People will do their best to meet you. You will receive plenty of handshakes and hugs, but most of the introductions should come later. I want to show you to your house before night, so refrain from engaging in any long conversations. I'm not saying to be rude though. Make sense?"

The teenagers nodded in unison. "Yes, sir, that makes complete sense. Thanks for the warning."

"All right, good." Holder smiled and grabbed the lever of the door. "And welcome to Australia." He threw the door open and stepped out onto the boarding ramp. Jason and Michaela took a deep breath and then followed him closely, exiting the plane and being overwhelmed with the cool spring air.

The first thing that Jason noticed distinctly was the magnitude of attention he and Michaela were receiving. Just as Holder had predicted, hundreds of people had gathered around the plane, and the vast majority of those people were pointing at the two Americans and talking. The attention was more exciting than threatening, however, so Jason didn't mind it.

Holder cupped both of his hands around his mouth and yelled out, "Can I have your attention?" The enormous crowd continued talking for several seconds, but eventually it was overtaken by silence, so Holder continued. "As you all know, for the last five months, my rescue team and I have been in America trying to save any survivors. We have seen many horrible things and experienced some things that nobody should go through, but still the mission was a success." He paused briefly and coughed after talking so loudly. "Out of every city we explored, we only found two survivors, but they are two great teenage kids. Ladies and gentlemen, meet our newest additions to the colony. This is Jason and Michaela." He turned to them and whispered, "Wave."

Following instructions, the two teenagers raised their hands and waved at the enormous sea of people. There was a brief moment of silence, and then a roar of cheers and applause broke loose. They instantly felt welcomed. This new place had already become their home.

The group slowly proceeded down the exit ramp and into the large crowd. The people parted down the middle, but not far enough away that Jason and Michaela were out of reach. Some of the colonists reached out and patted the newcomers on the back, and others shook their hands. Even more called out to both the teenagers and Holder.

Jason looked behind him. The crowd of people had once again enclosed behind them, but the plane was still in sight. The other campers were visible exiting, carrying bags and other supplies. Some of the colonists were boarding the plane and assisting in unloading it. The colony of Australia seemed to be very active and busy. Ahead of them, more buildings were becoming visible. Holder pointed to a distant row of buildings and said, "We are going over there." He had to speak loudly to be heard over the talkative crowd.

Michaela asked, "Where are we going to stay?"

Once again, Holder pointed in the same direction and announced, "You'll be living in a house over there, but let's get out of this crowd before I try to explain just so I can be heard well."

With that, the three continued forward, weaving through the busy street until they had gotten away from the majority of the people, and the bustling feeling somewhat diminished. By now, they were walking on some sort of a street. However, it had no cars on it, either operational or abandoned. There were several people on the street, but not as many as there had been when they had first arrived. At the end of most of the blocks were men standing behind vending booths, trading articles of clothing, food, and other various things.

Jason began to look at the buildings beside the street. As he paid more attention to them, he began noticing more peculiarities. The building to his right was pink in color. The architecture was unusual, but Jason knew he had seen it somewhere before. From the top of the large building hung the flag of Spain, and seeing that made Jason realize that the building was adobe. It had a large front entrance into which walked both a Hispanic man and his apparent young daughter.

Jason asked, "So why is this building so…um… Spanish?"

Holder smiled and replied, "I figured someone as observant as you would notice." He gestured with his hand around the large area. "This is the part of the colonies where our people live. All the buildings started out the same, but it was the idea of our architects to mix in a little cultural creativity to the apartments." He then pointed to the pink building. "For example, this building was renovated before my rescue mission to Spain. All of the survivors that we brought back with us from Spain live in this apartment building. I believe there are thirty-seven of them."

"That's really interesting," Jason said. "So how many different buildings are there?"

Holder was obviously calculating in his head. He answered, "The vast majority of the apartments are the original ones for the Australians, but regarding the different cultural buildings, I believe there are nine.

Spanish, French, Polish…" He began listing off various nationalities but trailed off. "I guess the specifics don't really matter though. Just wait until you see yours."

The statement hung in the air for several seconds before Jason said, "Wait, are you saying the United States has its own apartment building?"

Now Holder pointed again but in a more specific area. Straight ahead, there was a large building at the end of the street. The building was just coming into clear view now, and in front of it a large flagpole stretched into the sky. At the tip of the pole flapped a red, white, and blue flag that Jason and Michaela both recognized.

Michaela let out a low whistle. "That's the American building? It's so big!"

Her observation was correct. The building was three stories tall with a big fountain in the lawn in front of it. It was brickwork, beautifully constructed with many windows overlooking the street. Jason shook his head. "It is fantastic! Who is living in it?"

The question had an obvious answer. "I am," Holder stated. "And now you will be the only two others in the building with me."

The thought was exciting to both the teenagers, apart from it meaning they were the last of the Americans left. Jason said, "Let's go look inside."

From across the street came an excited outburst. "If it isn't the amazing Holder!" The words were well pronounced, and the voice was obviously male. Jason looked in the direction the words had come from in an attempt to locate their source. He identified the man, who was dressed in a black jacket over a white V-neck with jeans. The man had a thin goatee and a wily smile. A dirty baseball cap was pulled down over his disheveled hair, but his green eyes seemed to radiate intelligence.

Holder instantly began walking toward the man. "Shade, it's been a while, buddy." They shook hands and clapped each other on the back like teammates before Holder turned and waved toward the two teenagers. "C'mere, Shade, I have someone that I'd like you to meet."

The men walked back across the street and to where the teenager stood. Holder's friend shook both of their hands and introduced himself. "I'm Thomas Shade. May I ask who you fine children are?"

Jason and Michaela introduced themselves, and Holder added, "You are talking to the only two surviving Americans that we found during the rescue mission, Shade."

Shade whistled, impressed. "That's quite an achievement, outliving the entire American population. Are you going to teach us some of your tricks?"

"You can't teach luck," Jason commented.

"Oh, I'm sure there is much more to it than just luck." Shade looked into Jason's eyes, and Jason felt as if the man was somehow reading his thoughts and emotions. "I don't believe in luck anyway. Everything happens for a reason, I figure."

Holder added, "Shade here is very high up in the Australian colony. He was elected to serve right under the prime minister and is probably the most intelligent man that you will ever meet in your life. He is also the one that I told you about who led the team that discovered the cure."

Shade noticed both the teenagers questioningly running their eyes over him again and smiled. "I'm sorry I didn't dress the part. I just got out of a meeting and already changed for the night, but I'm really not fond of formality anyway."

"That's fine," Michaela said. "I think I might have dressed nice twice in my life."

"How old are you both?"

Michaela answered, "We are both eighteen, but my birthday was only two weeks ago."

Shade seemed to be calculating something in his head, but he didn't share anything. Finally, he asked, "Are you two siblings, friends, or a couple?"

Jason responded to this one, "We are a couple. I had a brother, but he was lost to the creepers in an attack about three months ago. We would have been killed too, but Holder saved us."

"Holder is a very heroic man," Shade said. "Everyone I know loves him." After this, he shook hands once again. "I'm really sorry, but I best go because I have plans to meet some of my friends tonight and grab some drinks. We got a bunch of stuff to talk about. I'm really excited about getting to know you two further, though. I suspect we will be seeing a lot of each other."

The four people exchanged farewells and Shade set off into the night. The group continued on, and five minutes later they had made it through the street and to the large apartment structure for the American survivors.

Holder led the teenagers inside through the beautifully crafted wooden door and into a large room filled with furniture, two televisions, a pool table, and a large book shelf full with countless old books. "Welcome to our house, this is the living room." he declared. "I think you will really like it here, so let's have a look around. I want to show you a few things you might find interesting."

He walked farther into the living room, and Jason and Michaela followed. They seemed to be walking toward the bookshelf when Michaela stopped and pointed to a framed piece of parchment on the wall. She looked pale. "Oh my gosh, is that the…"

"Yes, that is the original Declaration of Independence." Holder confirmed. "Two years ago, I took a group of nine back to the United States for a month in an attempt to preserve some of the treasures of my nation. The trip was short because there were far too many creepers, but we managed to bring home some American treasures. I was really hoping to find survivors as well, but that didn't happen. I guess I have never told you that story."

Jason's eyes were also fixed on the famous document, hanging casually on the wall in the living room of his new home. He read over the first few lines in amazement. "I can't believe this."

Holder laughed. "I really believe it's special, which is why I went back for it. You two should see the constitution. It's in my bedroom in a case right below *American Gothic*. We dropped by Chicago for that painting on the way home." He continued forward now. "Come and look at the bookshelf."

Michaela hurried over, pulling Jason by the hand. "Is there a secret passage?"

"Not quite." Holder chuckled, running his eyes along the books. He selected one and took it from the shelf and handed it to Jason. "This is a first edition, 1851 copy of Herman Melville's *Moby Dick* in very good condition. I even read it too, but it took me a *whale* of a time." He looked at the teenagers. "That was a pun."

The humor was missed because both Jason and Michaela had begun poring over the old books. There were works by American greats, including a first edition copy of *Tom Sawyer*. Finally, Jason spoke. "Where did you get all these?"

"We, um, *borrowed* them from the Library of Congress. A few of these books were originally owned by Thomas Jefferson." The entire house was beginning to feel like a museum to the teenagers. "But it's getting late, so I should probably show you to your rooms for the night. Tomorrow will be a big day."

They left the living room, went down a hallway, and began ascending a large spiraling stairwell. Jason asked, "What did you mean when you said that tomorrow will be a big day?"

After reaching the second flight of stairs, Holder began walking down a hallway with doors to apartments on each side. He explained. "After every rescue mission, I have to give a speech about how it went, what we found, and stuff of that nature. It is open to all colonists. The speech is tomorrow. I would really like you two to get on stage with me. Before you object, let me tell you that you don't have to talk, but if you stand with me, then people will be able to identify you both. So what do you say?"

"That's not a problem at all," Jason answered for both Michaela and himself.

"Fantastic, the meeting will be tomorrow morning after breakfast." Holder stopped outside a room and opened the door. "Here, this can be your room if you want. I'm right across the hall. If you'd rather have more privacy, feel free to pick any room you want. Nobody lives on the third floor obviously." He chuckled.

"No, this is absolutely perfect." Michaela wandered into the room, and Jason followed her. "Thank you so much for everything, Holder."

"No problem," their friend kindly responded. "Your bags will be dropped off here in the morning, and we will go find you some more clothes tomorrow. I will leave you two alone for the night, but in the morning meet me in the living room, and we will go to breakfast. You have a television, but it only plays DVDs, which we can rent some for you tomorrow. Also, there is a radio, and the Australian colony set up an AM station, which should be preset. Now good night!" He closed the door to the room, leaving Jason and Michaela alone inside.

The room was very large. There was a refrigerator and microwave, a warm shower in the bathroom, a queen-sized bed, and a television mounted on the opposite wall. Transitioning from the life at the camp back into a life with electricity and air condition was a wonderful change. Jason turned on the radio that sat on the nightstand, and a song he had never heard before began playing. He tiredly dropped down on the bed, and Michaela sat down beside him.

"Well, we made it," she said.

"Thank goodness, Jason answered. "I'm just so ready to try to get Drake back though."

"I know you are, but that will happen soon enough. For now, let's try to get some sleep. Tomorrow sounds like it will be a busy day."

"Yeah, good idea."

Michaela stood up and turned off the lights for the night, thankful brightness could be restored with the flip of a switch. Both of the tired teenagers lay down in the bed, forgetting about their problems and the horrible events they had been through over the last six years of their lives. Temporarily at peace, the young couple fell asleep.

6

When Jason awoke the next morning, Michaela was already sitting up in the bed beside him and staring out the room's window, which was to their right. The window offered a pleasant view of the colony. A deep-orange morning sun was carrying in the new day, peeking above the horizon from behind the various-sized buildings. A few people were walking down the carless streets of the colony as the beautiful sunrise stretched across the sky.

"Good morning," Michaela said. She rubbed Jason on the head, fixing his hair.

Jason blinked his eyes and stretched in the bed. "What time is it?"

Michaela consulted with the clock that hung on the wall opposite the bed. "It is almost seven o'clock."

"Oh, I can still sleep then!" Jason laid his head down on the pillow.

"Oh, no you aren't." Michaela shook him. "We are going to go eat some breakfast with Holder."

Jason resisted at first, but finally gave in. He sat up beside Michaela. "Do you think Holder is even awake this early?"

"I know he is," Michaela answered. "I went down to the living room about an hour ago, and he was already up and reading a handwritten poem by Robert Frost."

"That is absolutely amazing," Jason said.

"I know! It's so neat that he has such rare poetry."

"No, I mean it was amazing that he was up before six o'clock in the morning." Jason swung his body and put his feet on the floor beside the bed. He stood up and turned to Michaela. "C'mon. You are the one who wants to go to breakfast this early, anyways." On his way out of the room, he spotted his bag that he packed in the settlement. It was leaning against the wall.

Michaela must have noticed his gaze because she said, "Oh, yeah, I forgot to tell you that I brought our stuff up here. Do you want to change into something before we leave?"

Upon looking at Michaela again, Jason realized that she had changed clothes. He took a few minutes to go into the bathroom and change into clean clothes that he got out of out of his bag. He put on a pair of dark jeans and a V-neck shirt that looked more formal than what he had been wearing.

"You look really nice, Jase," Michaela told him as he walked back into the room.

"Thanks." The teenagers walked into the hallway. Michaela followed him down the stairwell and into the living room of the large house where Holder sat in one of the chairs. He was dressed in a casual shirt with jeans on, far less militaristic than anything Jason had ever seen him in. Holder looked up from his reading and greeted, "Good morning! Did you sleep well?"

"We did," Jason answered.

"Are you ready for breakfast?" Holder stood as if the teenagers had already answered and began walking across the living room to the building's front door.

They both followed Holder out of the building. Jason asked, "So, where do we eat breakfast?"

They stepped into the crisp morning air and began walking across the well-kept lawn. Holder explained. "About a block and a half away is a cafeteria that provides meals for everyone. It serves breakfast, lunch, and supper, along with snacks twenty-four seven. There is a nacho and soup bar between meals."

"That actually sounds really good," Michaela said.

"It is. The cafeteria does very well here in the settlement. None of the houses even have kitchens, but all of the rooms have microwaves and refrigerators for keeping snacks from the cafeteria."

After Holder finished the explanation, the group continued forward in silence. They made pleasant conversation during breakfast in the cafeteria, however, and the breakfast itself was very good: an enormous buffet set up with eggs, bacon, sausage, different pastries, and other breakfast foods and beverages. They ate for almost half an hour before Holder stood up and said, "Are you ready for some excitement?"

The cafeteria was beginning to fill up by now as more and more people were waking up and getting around to eating.

The teenagers followed Holder across the crowded room to set their trays in a large bin where the used utensils were being placed. The group then headed out of the cafeteria, fighting against the waves of people that kept rolling in. When they were finally outside, Jason asked, "So where are we going now?"

Holder led the group down the street in the opposite direction of their house. "Remember the assembly I told you about? That starts in an hour, so that is where we are headed."

Neither Jason nor Michaela had any idea of what to expect. They followed Holder, too busy studying the local buildings to carry a thoughtful conversation. After a solid ten minutes of walking, the group of three arrived at a large park somehow tucked away right in the heart of the colony. The park was large and flat with several benches, trees, and light poles arranged around a sidewalk that gently curved across the grass. At the far end of the park, Jason could see a large elevated platform set up in an open clearing. The platform was wooden and about three feet high. A tall red curtain had been hung between two tall poles and was being used as a backdrop.

Holder pointed at the platform. "That is where I'll give the short speech about the rescue mission. There are a couple of chairs that you can sit in while I talk, and if you don't mind, then I'd like to formally introduce you to the colonists. Minister Gordon will probably give a short speech too. He usually does. Does everything sound all right?"

"Yes," Jason said. "We don't have a problem with going up on the stage with you. How long until the meeting starts, and when will people start showing up?"

Holder looked at his wristwatch. "People will probably start arriving here in about half an hour, and then we will start probably fifteen minutes after that."

At this time, a man stepped out from behind the backdrop and walked around the stage. He was tall and slender with a thin face and a balding head. Round wire spectacles were perched on the man's nose. Upon spotting Holder and the teenagers, he raised his hand in a welcoming gesture, greeting them. "Holder, welcome back, my friend!"

Holder walked toward the man and smiled, calling out, "Minister Gordon! It has been a while." The teenagers followed, realizing that they were in the company of the leader of the settlement.

Gordon shook both Jason and Michaela's hand respectively as soon as he had greeted Holder. He said, "I'm assuming you must be the Americans that Holder told me about. It is such an honor." He spoke softly and seemed genuinely pleased to meet the newcomers. "I am Minister Jeffery Gordon. What are your names?"

"I'm Jason, and this is Michaela."

Minister Gordon smiled. "Ah, young love." He looked between the teenagers knowingly before continuing. "You have no idea how impressed I was when I heard the story of how you two survived the apocalypse at such a young age. That was quite an impressive act, and I would love having the opportunity to further discuss the matter with you over lunch if you would accompany me to my house after the end of the meeting here. What do you say?"

Jason looked first to Holder and then to Michaela. He certainly hadn't been expecting a dinner invitation. Knowing not what else to say and not wanting to refuse the request of the man who was indirectly responsible for saving his life, Jason agreed. "That is no problem at all. We would be honored to be your guests."

Minister Gordon bit his lower lip, a look of contemplation on his face. "When I say this, know that I am not trying to be hurtful or cruel, but I would really like to discuss losing your brother Drake. Mr. Holder told me of the unfortunate circumstances."

The words stung Jason's heart. He also still hadn't gotten over losing his brother. He just tried not to think about it. "All right, we can talk about that." His voice had not sounded as solid as he had hoped.

Minister Gordon smiled. "Don't look so sad. I would like to discuss my hopes for potentially curing your brother. It is a very interesting topic, and I think you might know some things that could come in useful. We can help each other."

Jason paused, weighing the words and considering them. He licked his lips and took a deep breath, trying not to become too hopeful. "So you mean there is a way that we can maybe save Drake?" Deep down, he had never let go of the hope of saving his brother, especially after Holder had mentioned the cure. Nonetheless, he felt strange voicing the tiny hope for the first time and not wanting his insecurities to get the best of him.

Gordon, still smiling, nodded and replied, "There is certainly a chance that we can save your brother. I will be more than happy to explain during lunch, my boy." The minister put his hand on Jason's shoulder and gave it a gentle squeeze before continuing. "But I think we best table this discussion for now, seeing as people are beginning to arrive for the assembly."

As Gordon left, Jason turned around to see at least a hundred people approaching the stage from various directions. He had been so absorbed in what the discussion he had failed to notice the obvious rise in noise level. He felt Michaela grab him by the hand from behind, so he turned back around to face her. She was smiling up at him. "What Minister Gordon said is fantastic news, Jason! We are going to get your brother back."

He smiled but replied, "I still can't get my hopes up. I don't know how we'd even find Drake again. I want him back so badly, but it just seems impossible."

Holder, who had been listening in, returned, "Don't give up, kid. We can do this. Know that I will do anything I can to help you get Drake back."

"Thanks, Holder."

"No problem. We better get up on the stage though. The scheduled starting time is in fifteen minutes."

With that, the three set off, pushing through the gathering crowd of people until they had reached the stage, which they ascended. Jason and Michaela sat down on two chairs toward the left side of the stage, while Holder went and stood by the podium.

After several minutes, the audience had grown considerably. Looking out across the spectators, Jason asked Michaela, "How many people do you think are out there?"

She looked around the sea of people who had assembled so quickly and said, "It's hard to tell. They need to stop moving! I would guess anywhere between twelve hundred to fifteen hundred." The estimate seemed accurate to Jason.

Within another couple minutes, the minister joined them on the stage, and the large assembly of people instantly fell silent. Gordon strode across the stage to the podium, by which Holder was standing. The two exchanged a few inaudible words and a handshake before Gordon turned to the podium and leaned into the microphone. "Good morning, ladies and gentlemen." His voice was firm despite the vast amount of people watching him. "I'm very glad you all have decided to spend the morning with us as Mr. Holder shares the events and information discovered on the latest rescue mission to America." He looked toward Holder. "This man has led over a dozen rescue missions and saved countless lives. Please join me in a round of applause for our hero."

A thunderous applause erupted from the hundreds of people in the audience. It lasted for several seconds before finally dying down. Michaela leaned in toward Jason to be heard, saying, "This entire park is full. I'm amazed at how many people came out to hear this speech."

Jason nodded but asked, "Well, what else are they going to do?"

"Good point."

Gordon spoke again. "I have decided that the mission Mr. Holder just arrived from will be the last rescue mission in search of any more survivors. The risk-to-reward is not nearly as great as it was when we were bringing back forty survivors." A murmur came from among the audience. "That being said, this mission was just as much as an accomplishment as the first one because lives were saved." Gordon looked back at Holder and nodded before concluding. "But I haven't gone anywhere or saved any lives. I'm not the hero that this fine man is, so it is not my place to tell you the stories or share the information he's gathered. Please put your hands together one more time for James Holder and his team."

Holder smiled and waved toward the audience before stepping to the microphone and opening with, "It's good to be back up here. There were a few times on that last mission that I didn't know if I'd ever be back in this fine colony." The statement received the desired effect, getting many gasps from throughout the audience. He continued, "That being said, I enjoyed every single minute of it, and it was so rewarding to bring two fine teenagers back here. Ladies and gentlemen, meet Jason and Michaela." He turned around and swung his arm toward the teenagers, who stood up and waved gingerly toward the audience.

Another explosion of cheering came. Jason whispered, "I think creepers are less scary than this. There are so many people!"

She laughed, and they sat down a few seconds later, causing the applause to fade. Holder spoke into the microphone. "Those are two of the finest teens I've ever met. They have survived the apocalypse from the age of thirteen. Can you even imagine that?" He paused shortly for the audience to process the words before beginning his recollection. "My men and I set up camp in the state of Georgia and sent helicopters to the largest cities of the United States. We saw hundreds of creepers, but only two humans." Jason noticed that Holder failed to mention the crazed man that arrived on the last day at camp, but that was for the good of the people there. The story continued. "I was personally on the helicopter that found these two and know that I'm not exaggerating by saying they didn't have much time left. We were flying to Miami when we spotted the largest group of creepers I'd ever seen—over two hundred—traveling in a pack to the ocean. As we got closer, we could tell the creepers were pursuing two humans, so we dropped in altitude and fired several rounds into the beach to scare the creepers into retreat."

Jason thought back to that very moment, trying to remember exactly how he had felt. It was at that instant that he and Michaela had discovered the creepers were not the enemy, but only unfortunate people who were sick. Losing his brother had been the primary factor leading to the dramatic revelation. Since that day, his entire view of the beasts had been revolutionized. He would never look at them the same way.

Holder continued the story. "From what I've been told, there had been a small society established in Miami. It had been built in an underground parking garage and was fairly close to discovering a cure when the creeper test subjects somehow had gotten loose and infected the entire establishment. Jason and Michaela were the only two who managed to escape." He paused, then said in a more solemn voice, "Jason had a brother named Drake who had been with him through everything, but he was lost to the creepers only minutes before my helicopter arrived."

Jason was sniffling as if he was going to cry, but he fought back the tears. Michaela leaned in and put an arm around him and grabbed his hand.

Over the next thirty minutes, Holder shared a few more stories from the latest rescue mission but then finally concluded by saying, "Please make Jason and Michaela feel welcomed in our society. If you haven't been lucky enough to meet them yet, then you need to. They are amazing kids. Please give them a hand one more time." The applause came and left, and then Holder finished. "I hope we will soon have at least one more addition to the settlement. I have promised Jason that we will get his brother back, and that is a promise that I intend to keep."

From his seat, Jason smiled widely while more applause came from the audience. Even Minister Gordon put his hands together at this. This time, the cheering didn't cease until the minister shook Holder's hand once again before stepping up to the microphone and speaking over the audience. "Now wasn't that an inspiration? I can speak for the entire population when I say that we are blessed for such a heroic and determined man like Mr. Holder."

Holder turned to face the teenagers and gestured for them to walk to the front of the stage with him. Jason looked at Michaela and shook his head. "He's got to be kidding."

Michaela stood and grabbed Jason by the hand before tugging him to his feet. "Oh, come on. You'll be fine."

He reluctantly followed her to Holder, who leaned down and said, "Stand here and wave at the people. They need to get a good look at you."

The teenagers did as told, while Gordon dismissed the meeting. "Thank you all for coming out and for the things you do every day to help this colony succeed. I hope you all have a great day, and that's all we have." He waved farewell to the people who were already beginning to disperse in different directions, and then he turned the microphone off and sighed.

Over the noise of the chattering from the crowd, Holder said, "I think that went well."

"I do too," said Gordon. He walked to the teenagers and said, "Thanks for standing up here with us. I'd imagine that can be nerve-racking the first time."

Jason was about to agree, but Michaela interjected. "No, it was kind of fun!"

Gordon smiled. "I really like you two. I can already tell." He looked out into the quickly receding tide of people walking away from the stage and then turned back to the teenagers. "Now would you be ready to join me for lunch and a discussion?" He stopped and looked at Holder. "You are more than welcome to join us too, Mr. Holder. Shade is going to be there as well."

Holder shook his head. "Thank you a lot, but I have a few things that I need to do."

"All right, that is no problem." Gordon smiled at Holder. "Thanks again for all that you do." They shook hands, and then Gordon looked at the kids. "Let's get a move on, I think you will be very interested to hear what I want to discuss."

As they were walking away, Holder called out, "Have fun, guys! I will talk to you later."

Not wanting to wait any longer than they had too, Jason and Michaela followed the minister off of the stage. Despite the many surprises that they had already encountered in Australia, neither one of them could imagine the news that they were soon to be told.

7

The walk through the city was fairly short in distance, yet it seemed to take a while because the minister was frequently stopped by many of the colonists. He exchanged smiles, words, and handshakes with them, showing the teenagers why he was so beloved among his people.

After traveling down a long street and then turning right onto a side street, the minister gestured to the large house ahead of them. "That is my house."

Jason let out a low whistle. "It's really nice." The house was surrounded by a tall wrought-iron fence with a large black gate in the front, opening up to a paved walkway that wound up to the front door of the large two-story house surrounded by trimmed hedges and a decorative fountain in the center of the ornate front yard. A cursive letter G was cast on both sides of the gate.

Gordon smiled. "I am really blessed. I did not ask for any of this, but I was given this all by the fine people here. They built everything for me."

"From what I have heard, you are the reason that this society survived, so the people probably feel like they owe their lives to you," said Michaela. "You are the people's hero."

As they continued walking, Gordon nodded. "Please don't think that I am being arrogant because that is not what I am intending." He hesitated but then said, "But the people love me just because of what I have done in the past. I won the election just because of my history. Sometimes I feel guilty because I'm only riding on the coattails of success."

"From what I've heard from Holder, it sounds like you are doing a fine job in leading this colony. You are respected. I could tell from the assembly." This came from Jason as he followed Gordon through the front gate and up the paved pathway.

Gordon chuckled. "Well, your words mean a lot to me. I try my hardest to lead to the best of my ability, but I have great help. I don't know if you have met Thomas Shade, but he has been there every step of the way. He is a brilliant man and a great leader, who is second-in-command in the colony."

"We have met him," Michaela said. "Holder introduced us."

"He seemed like a very interesting person," commented Jason.

Gordon took keys from his pocket and unlocked the front door while explaining. "When I ran for minister, it was against Thomas. I won but made him my assistant because of how brilliant he was, and he was very appreciative of the opportunity. He will be eating lunch with us today, but he eats with me every day."

The minister pushed the front door of his house open and stepped to the side so the teenagers could enter. Jason gratefully walked into the house, and Michaela followed behind. The door opened into the great room, which was unbelievably lavish. A fire was ablaze in the hearth and flooded the room with a warm, welcome feeling. A finger of a flame seemed to curl inward, as if gesturing Jason to come inside. Two ornate wall clocks hung on opposite walls, and the room had several pieces of fine leather furniture. The far wall was lined with a bookshelf, and a small table was underneath it. On the table was a reading light and an open book.

Gordon could somehow tell where Jason was looking, and he asked, "Do you read much?"

"I do. It was my only source of entertainment for a long time," responded Jason. "My brother and I read all of the time when we were in New York."

The minister smiled. "There is something to be said about a well-read man." He gestured to his fancy suit and said, "If you'll excuse me for a couple of minutes, I will go change into something a little less formal before lunch." He nodded across the room. "The doorway over there is the restroom, so you can wash up, and then the dining room is right there." He pointed before saying, "If you have a seat in there, my cook will get you drinks."

"I could get used to this," exclaimed Michaela.

Jason glanced at her in disapproval. "What she means is that we appreciate this very much, Minister

Gordon. Your hospitality is very kind, and I am eager for our lunchtime discussion."

"That excites me." Gordon shook the teenagers' hands one more time before saying, "You are two of the most polite teenagers I've been around in a very long time. I will go change and meet you in the dining room for dinner—or do you Americans say 'lunch'?" He laughed and turned around, disappearing down a hallway in the large house.

After standing in place for a few seconds, Michaela said, "You heard the man. Let's wash up so that we can eat!" She walked to the bathroom and halfheartedly washed her hands before Jason followed suit. Once they had cleaned up, they went to the dining room, where they found a long and beautiful mahogany table. The table had six seats—two on each side and one on each end—along with a decorative cornucopia centerpiece and orange placemats. Jason and Michaela sat beside each other on one side of the table and awkwardly looked around the room.

Shortly thereafter, the sound of footsteps came toward the dining room. Jason looked at Michaela. "This must be the chef."

They both turned to the dining room's entryway and were surprised to see the cheery figure of Thomas Shade enter the room. He spotted the teenagers sitting at the table and looked quizzically at them at first but then grinned, "Well, I didn't know we were expecting company, but I have been really looking forward to getting to know you two fine young people." He shook Jason's hand and then lightly took Michaela's hand and pulled it to his lips, kissing it slightly. "It is an honor to be in the presence of the young heroes I have heard so much about." Shade walked to the other side of the table and sat down.

Jason looked at the man. Shade's eyes gleamed with intelligence. "I have heard a lot about you as well, from Holder and Gordon."

Shade laughed slightly and teased. "I hope you heard good things, but I doubt it." He turned his head to the doorway and called out, "Ms. Martha, are you here?"

Seconds later, a plump and smiling woman who was wearing an apron stepped into the room. She seemed pleased to see them and said, "Thomas, how are you, my dear boy?" She looked to the teenagers and cooed, "I have heard so much about you, and I'm so proud to be serving you. What would you like for drinks? Tea? Coffee?"

"Tea, please," both Jason and Michaela answered in unison.

"And the usual black coffee for you, Thomas?"

"Yes, ma'am."

The cheerful woman left the room, only to return a minute later with four drinks. She distributed them appropriately and sat a large glass of lemonade on the placemat of the spot where Gordon would presumably be sitting. She vanished again and returned this time with various dishes of food that she began setting around the middle of the table.

She had just finished setting the table when Gordon walked into the room. He was wearing a white button-down shirt and black slacks, so he still looked formal, but not as much so as before. He praised the meal on the table, saying, "Martha, dinner looks fantastic as usual." She thanked him and left the room, while Gordon sat down at the head of the table and took a long drink from his lemonade. He then opened his arms and said, "Please help yourself."

Not needing to be told twice, the teenagers filled their plates with different meats, vegetables, and pastas that had been set before them as Gordon greeted Shade. They began eating in silence for a brief moment.

After a moment, Gordon told them, "I hope you enjoy the meal, and if you need anything, just ask. Let's get to talking though. We have a lot to discuss." He had a large slab of turkey on his plate, of which he cut and took a bite. He chewed thoughtfully before asking, "I suppose the best way to begin is by asking if either of you have been inoculated against the virus. Did Holder or anyone else give you the vaccine once you arrived?"

Jason shook his head. "No. Holder mentioned the vaccine, but neither of us have received it yet."

"Given as busy as you two have been since arriving, I'm not very surprised." He looked to Shade. "I have two of the vaccines here if Thomas would agree to administer them to you after dinner. Do you mind?"

"It would be my honor," Shade answered.

"Good." Gordon took another bite of turkey and then chased it with more lemonade. He licked his lips and said, "There is one more matter I'd like to discuss, but I'm really not sure how to ask." He looked to Shade for advice but received none, so he simply stated, "Mr. Shade here has led a team of doctors in perfecting the cure and a way to administer it on a large scale, so we would like to send a rescue mission back to the United States in an attempt to save the people of Miami and get your brother back."

That was a lot of news to Jason, and he tried to digest what had been said. He asked, "So you want to cure the city of Miami? How on earth is that possible?"

Gordon replied, "Well, the details have not been completely worked out, but this seems like the perfect opportunity. Shade recently concluded his groundbreaking development in curing the virus on a large scale, and when we heard the story about your brother, we decided this might be the best time to test the cure."

Jason took a bite of his rice and pondered how he should respond before saying, "A rescue mission would be fantastic, especially if it saved my brother." He now looked to Michaela, who seemed to be thinking the same thing as him. "But if this mission is going back to the same place we just came from, can we go too? You know, as assistants?"

"That's exactly why I invited you to eat with us today," Gordon said. "I wanted to ask your for assistance on the mission. Would you consider it?"

Now the teenagers shared another glance and answered at the same time once again. "Definitely!"

Jason went on to ask, "Who will be leading this mission, if you don't mind my asking?" He scooped up more rice on his fork and took a bite and then said, "Wow, this is fantastic!"

Gordon chuckled. "I'm glad you are enjoying the meal." He took out a piece of paper from his pocket that was creased down the middle, unfolding it and studying it before answering, "In terms of the mission, Thomas has already agreed to lead it, and I intend to ask your friend Holder if he would consider coleading. The combination of both military and intellectual brilliance would give the mission the best chance for success that I can see."

Michaela said, "I love Holder to death, and you seem great too, Mr. Shade, so I couldn't think of two better leaders."

"I'm flattered," Shade commented, and he sounded sincere. "I have seven friends that I asked to join on the mission with me, and the rest of the members of our rescue team will hopefully be some of the same people that were on the rescue mission you just arrived from." He looked at both of the teenagers and then added, "This mission is going to be exciting for sure!"

"I have no doubts at all," Jason replied and then turned to Gordon. "You said that the cure has been perfected. Could you explain how it works?"

"Once again, that is a better question for Thomas. He is the brilliant mind who invented it, after all."

All eyes once again turned to Shade, who was wiping his mouth with a napkin. He set it down and licked his lips, obviously contemplating what he was going to say. Finally, he began, "I can try to explain this in a simple fashion because it is fairly groundbreaking science. I'm being honest, not boastful." He looked up at Jason. "I know you didn't have much formal schooling, but how familiar are you in the field of microbiology?"

Jason shook his head. "I have very limited knowledge."

Shade laughed in a friendly manner and joked. "I wish the same were true to me. Sometimes it's hard to get out of bed when I know I could pick up bacteria lethal enough to kill me on a doorknob or light switch." He paused. "But then I just consider the microorganisms living *inside* my bed and decide to get up." Continuing, Shade asked, "Do you know what bacteria are?"

"Yes."

"Good. Have either of you heard of genetic engineering?" At this, both of the teenagers shook their heads, so Shade explained. "Basically, it is just slightly modifying the DNA of microscopic cells and unicellular organisms so they can do something you want them to do. The best way I can simplify it is by saying that it's like programming living creatures."

"That's really neat." Jason was nearly done with his plate, so he sat his fork down and listened better to what Shade was saying.

"To create the cure for the disease, I worked with a small team of doctors to genetically engineer bacteria that could deactivate the virus within the host cell and then block the cells from further accepting the virus." He took a small pad of paper and a pen from his pocket and began an illustration to go along with what he was attempting to explain. "Many of the cells in the human body have tiny receptors on them." He drew short lines on the cells. "The microorganisms I genetically engineered block these receptors so that the virus can no longer attach." He drew the letter X on the end of the lines. "After the virus can no longer attach, it is excreted from the body, and the host is cured."

"That's amazing!" Michaela was legitimately impressed. "How did you come up with the idea?"

"A lot of reading, a lot of creativity, and a little luck." Shade folded the paper and put it away.

Jason asked, "So the cure has been tested?"

"It has, and it worked to unbelievable results," Shade responded. "It even cures more than the virus itself."

"What do you mean?"

Shade looked thoughtful again. "So far, the cure has been tested on seventeen people. All seventeen of them survived. That is not even the most interesting part, however. Two of the cured people had been diagnosed with terminal cancer before contracting the virus, but all traces of the cancer had vanished after they were cured. I'm not sure if this was sheer coincidence, or if there is a medical reason behind it, but I intend to look into the matter further."

Both Jason and Michaela finished their dinner, but Shade still had a few morsels of food on his plate. Not wanting the conversation to end, Jason asked, "How is this cure going to be given to an entire city?"

Shade answered the question with another question. "Have you ever heard of an endospore?" Jason shook his head. "An endospore is living bacteria that has been shut down and stays in a dormant state. It's asleep, so to speak." Jason nodded to show that he understood, so Shade continued, "I learned a process of heating the bacteria I genetically engineered to change them into an endosporic state. They make a tiny dust if you gather enough of them—I'm talking billions of these tiny endospores."

Michaela asked, "They are just tiny cells that are in hibernation?"

"Exactly!" Shade took another piece of paper from his pocket and held it up. On the parchment was the printed design for some sort of long metal cylinder. He looked very proud of it. "I call this the duster. It's an original design." Shade slid the parchment in front of the teenagers, and they studied it while he explained. "It's modeled after a crop duster, but it will be welded onto a helicopter, and the pilot will be able to make it release the microscopic endospores while the helicopter flies over the city. There are so many of them that the spores will literally go everywhere with the wind's assistance, and then they will be inhaled by all of the infected creepers. Within hours, everyone should be cured of the virus, and we will hand out supplies."

Jason said, "That sounds like an amazing plan, but will it work?"

Gordon nodded with certainty. "Anything Shade creates works perfectly."

"Except my election campaign." Shade teased.

Having finished dinner, all four people stood. Gordon left the room for a few seconds and reentered with two syringes filled with a clear fluid. He handed them to Shade. "This is the vaccine."

Jason and Michaela both were amazed by the concept of being made immune to the virus that had ravaged the earth, and in seconds, the inoculations were made, and the empty syringes were disposed. Shade elaborated by telling them, "I just injected the genetically engineered bacteria into your bloodstream. They will block the virus from connecting to your cell receptors, but a creeper could still tear you in half, so you'll have to be careful on the mission regardless."

They all made their way to the front door, and Jason said, "Speaking of the mission, how long until it will take place?"

Gordon's answer was stunning. "The plans have not been made, but if Holder and the others will agree to participate, then I hope that it can set off in just a couple of days. Tomorrow we'll hold a meeting at noon to discuss the finer details, assuming everyone agrees to participate, and I would like both of you to come."

"Not a problem," Jason said. He was thrilled with the potential of the mission leaving so soon, especially with his brother's life depending on it. He and Michaela bid Shade and Gordon farewell and set off into the heart of the colony hand in hand.

They walked in silence for a few minutes, digesting the information that they had been overloaded with. Michaela broke the silence by saying, "I'm so happy we are going to get Drake back!"

Jason smiled too but then fought back doubts of skepticism. "I just hope nothing goes wrong."

Michaela looked him sternly in the face and shook her head. "I'm confident that this will go well. With all of the despair and trouble that we have had in our lives, I don't see what else could go wrong."

"I guess we'll just have to find out."

8

At the same time on the next day, the teenagers were walking on the same street but in the opposite direction. Holder walked ahead of them, leading the way. He had been asked by Minister Gordon to colead the mission with Shade the previous afternoon, and he had eagerly accepted the invitation. In fact, Shade, Gordon, and Holder had met for at least an hour and a half that night and discussed the plans for the mission, and Gordon had told the teenagers that they should begin packing for the trip back to America.

As they continued down the street, Jason asked, "Where is this meeting being held? Is it going to be in Gordon's house?"

"No." Holder shook his head. "There is a conference room beside the minister's house where all the important meetings take place." By now, Gordon's magnificent house was within sight, and to the right side of it, another smaller building was visible that Jason had not noticed the previous day. Holder said, "That building right there is where the meeting will take place."

A group of eight men came into sight. They too were walking to the meeting house, but from the opposite direction. Michaela, eyeing the group, asked, "Isn't that Shade?"

She was correct. Shade was walking ahead of the other men, obviously leading the pack. He was wearing slacks, a button-down shirt, and a confident smile. Shade spotted Holder and the teenagers, so he called out, "James! How are you all today?"

Holder and the teenagers approached, and Shade shook all of their hands. Holder said, "It's good to see you, Shade. I'm looking forward to going on this mission with you. I've always thought that we would make a great team."

"I completely agree!" Shade stepped back and waved toward the men following him. "These are the friends I asked to join us on the mission."

One person in particular caught Jason's eye. A black man standing beside Shade was enormously tall. He stood at least six foot and seven inches, with long wild dreadlocks pulled back behind his head in a band. He wore a tank top to reveal bulging muscles and a sleeve of tattoos on both arms. The man stepped forward and shook hands with the teenagers, introducing himself. "My name is Navarro Truman." His voice was a deep rumble. "It is nice to meet you. I have heard so much about all of you from Shade."

Truman's enormous hand swallowed Jason's as they shook. He looked up at the towering man and jokingly said, "In a battle against creepers, you'd be the one I'd want on my side."

Truman laughed, and Shade said, "That was what I thought as well. Truman here is quite a specimen." He patted the big man on the back and then checked his watch before saying, "Let's get inside, the meeting is about to begin."

The group of people walked inside the meeting house to find a very long table with chairs on both sides, about half of which were full. Minister Gordon stood at the head of the table on the far side of the room. He was holding a list in front of him and continually glanced from the paper to the people who had just entered the building before proclaiming, "We are all here now, so let's begin." He smiled up at the newcomers and said, "Please, take a seat."

All of them did as told, filtering in among the people who were already seated. Most of those people were recognizable from the first rescue mission, including the enormous, jolly chef named Teddy. He waved at Jason, who returned the greeting as he followed Holder deeper into the room. They walked toward where the minister sat near the other end of the table and took the three seats closest to him on one side of the table. Shade, Truman, and another of Shade's friends sat opposite them.

Once everyone was sitting, the minster said, "I'm so thankful you all could come to this meeting with me and that all of you are willing to go on this rescue mission. You are heroes—every single one of you. It is missions like these that will be in the history books in five hundred years. I believe a round of applause is deserved for all of you." He put his hands together, and the other people in the room followed.

"He really has a way of inspiring people," Michaela whispered to Jason, who nodded his agreement.

Gordon continued, "As you all know, this mission is going to be led by both Holder and Shade." He looked at both of them in turn. "Thank you both from the bottom of my heart. I appreciate all of the planning you put into this, Thomas, and it means so much that you volunteered to go on such short notice, James."

Shade spoke up. "There is no need for thanks, Minister Gordon. I have been preparing this cure for so long that I am excited to finally have the opportunity to test it."

"I agree with Shade completely. Thanks is not necessary at all," said Holder. "This is a huge opportunity to make a positive difference, and if we just cure one single creeper, then the trip will be worth it to me."

"I'm so blessed to be working with both of you two men," Gordon reiterated. He finally sat down in the chair at the head of the table and turned to Shade. "Why don't you start explaining the details of the mission, Thomas? Everyone else, feel free to ask questions."

"All right." Shade had a notebook, and he consulted with it before beginning. "This mission is intended to be short. We leave tomorrow, and we are scheduled to be back in thirty days."

One of his men asked, "What is to happen if, for some reason, we are not back? What if something goes wrong?"

Shade was completely prepared for the question and offered a quick response. "There will be a three-day waiting period after the thirty days are up, and if we still haven't arrived, another plane will be sent to check on the mission."

The man who had asked the question nodded approvingly, but now one of the campers who had been on the first mission asked, "How do we get to Miami?" He looked to Holder. "The same way as last time?"

Holder answered, "Yes. We will fly out from here tomorrow and spend tomorrow night in San Francisco. From there we will fly to the camp we set up in Georgia, and we will move the supplies from the plane to the six trucks we left there, and Shade's dusting tool will be welded onto one of the three helicopters. We have extra fuel, so after spending the night in the Georgia camp, we will leave for Miami the next morning, taking the six trucks and the helicopter."

Shade took over again. "We will take clothes and food supplies for two hundred people. Once we reach Miami, we can always go to the local stores and gather more supplies as needed, but bringing items from here will be a very good start."

Holder interjected. "We need to remember these people will have nothing. Their clothes are tattered, and their belongings have been lost and scattered. Everything that they receive will have to be provided by us. We have to take soap, towels, toothpaste, anything that they could, by chance, need."

"Holder makes a great point." Shade approved. "These creepers are not going to be our enemies. Once we cure them, they will just be scared and confused people." He looked to Jason. "Holder also told me that there was a colony of survivors in Miami until the creepers overtook them. Can you estimate how many people were in this colony?"

All eyes were on Jason, and he swallowed. "Probably five hundred. Do you agree Michaela?"

"Yes, that is a good guess." Her voice was both calm and confident.

Now Shade asked, "And of that five hundred survivors, how many do you believe were transformed into creepers?"

Jason answered again, "Maybe three hundred tops. The entire settlement turned into a bloodbath, and many of both the humans and creepers were killed. That is when they got my brother…" His voice trailed off.

"We are going to get your brother back." Holder promised. "That is the reason for the urgency of this meeting. We want Drake back as soon as possible."

"You have no idea how much that means to me."

Shade studied his pad of paper and commented, "Even if there are three hundred creepers in the city, finding extra supplies won't be too pressing of a challenge, but I'd imagine that some of the creepers would've died by now." Jason tried to force this thought out of his mind. "Any more questions?"

Truman asked in his rumbling voice, "How are we going to house that many people?"

Holder said, "I know that this sounds very far-fetched, but we will take tents, and some of the people can live in the tents on the beach." There were murmurs throughout the room, but Holder said, "The tents will only be for about one hundred people, but keep in mind many of these people are from Miami and will have homes that they will want to return to." He scanned the room, obviously trying to find someone. "Where is Reginald?"

A short and blonde man raised his hand from the far end of the table. "Right here."

"Excellent," said Holder. "Reginald, as most of you know, is an electrician, and we will take a large generator that he can use to power a hotel. This might take a couple days to complete, but eventually we will have electricity, and maybe even water, in a hotel, and the people can move in there for the rest of the rescue phase."

"The rescue phase?" Michaela asked this question.

"Yes, the rescue phase." Holder turned to Gordon. "Do you care to explain? This part was your idea, after all."

"You are correct." Gordon paused and appeared to be thinking deeply. "After all of the creepers have been cured, there will obviously be far too many to bring back to our colony with one trip. They will have to get established enough to function on their own for the time it takes us to bring them to the colony."

A woman sitting beside Jason asked, "So will we need to stay with them for that entire time?"

"No." Gordon shook his head. "I think only one or two people should stay any additional time to help them get on their feet, and fortunately both Holder and Shade have volunteered for this task."

Holder added, "To help clarify, this mission was scheduled for thirty days. Theoretically, all of the infected humans should be cured by day ten, and for the next twenty days, we all will help them establish means of survival. After that, everyone but Shade and I will return back here. We will stay with the cured humans over the next two months while enough planes are sent to bring them back to the colony, and then we will return home."

Michaela poked Jason in the side and whispered, "Did you know he was staying behind?"

Jason shook his head. "I had no idea."

She said, "We should also volunteer to stay so we get to come back with Drake. I know how excited you are about having him back."

Jason could not prevent a huge grin from spreading across his face. "I honestly don't think you have any idea about how bad I want him back."

Shade, after citing his notes, began to explain something else. "Some of the people going on this mission have specific tasks and specialties. For example, one of my men named Maxwell is a welder, and his main job is to attach my duster onto the helicopter. Where are you, Max?" He looked down the table until he identified the man named Maxwell, a tall and athletic-looking man with dark hair and a goatee.

The rest of the meeting continued in this fashion, discussing the small details of the mission until every single thing had been ironed out. The group discussed subjects as broad as what they needed to pack and the food and drinks that Teddy should bring, but also they discussed things as specific as the brand of camping tents and sleeping bags that were preferred.

Jason counted twenty-five people who were going to be on the mission, just like the last. This included Shade and his seven friends, fourteen people who had been on the previous mission, including the teenagers, and two unfamiliar faces. Excluding himself and Michaela, he also counted twenty-one men and two women. Both women had a husband going on the mission.

Finally, after the final plans were made, Gordon dismissed by saying, "Once again, thank you so much for your assistance. You better set out so you can get to packing and say your farewells because the plane will leave tomorrow at noon. Once again, I am inspired by all of you men and women. It warms my heart to see such determination to do good."

The people in the room began to slowly file out, and Jason and Michaela accompanied Shade and Holder to the cafeteria for lunch. The group of four ate a quick meal, and Shade politely dismissed himself, saying he needed to go help his men with packing, leaving Holder and the teenagers alone.

Holder asked, "What are you two thinking? Are you nervous about this mission?"

"I'm trying my hardest to stay confident," Jason said. "And the meeting we just came from really helped. I feel like everything is planned out very well, and I think a great plan is a large component of success."

Holder laughed and replied, "I like that. Maybe I should get that painted on my wall at home or something." He adopted a more serious tone and said, "All jokes aside, I agree completely. Things are planned out very meticulously. I'm not saying that he's perfect, but I will say that things seem to always go the way that Shade plans them."

"I know exactly what you mean." Jason agreed. "From the little time I have spent around him, he strikes me as a winner, y'know? Shade seems like a brilliant mind and very creative thinker, and he is extremely charismatic. Just being around him makes me a little bit more confident in what we are doing."

"Yes, I've never met a person like him. This mission will go just as he wants it to, I promise. Your brother will be saved soon, Jason." Holder patted Jason on the back. "But we better go and get the rest of our stuff together." He stood, and the teenagers followed. They put the cafeteria trays away and set out. Nobody was talking, but all three of them were thinking about the important plane flights that were awaiting them and of the rescue mission at the end of the long journey that lay ahead.

9

The roads were in terrible condition, but Tanya had expected this. More than once, over the previous two days of driving, she had to stop the car and clear the road from trees and debris with Anna and JR. She had managed to fit eight five-gallon cans of gasoline in the trunk of the car and their belongings in the backseat beside JR.

Apart from the delays, the trip had gone smoothly, with no major surprises, and only a few creeper sightings throughout the entire trip. They had made it to Georgia, nearing the final destination of Miami, when Anna broke the silence that had overtaken the car while JR slept in the backseat. "What is that?" She pointed out the window.

Tanya looked in that direction, and in the dying light of day, she could see an open clearing in the woodlands to their left. The clearing wasn't empty, however. Instead, several large trucks were parked in an obviously organized row on the far side, and there were even multiple helicopters on the opposite side of the clearing. In the direct middle was what appeared to be a large fire pit, ashy and black.

"That looks like a campground," she said, slowing the car to a stop in the middle of the road. "Let's go check it out. We need to refill fuel anyway. We are just about out."

Anna turned around in her seat and shook JR, saying, "Wake up, champ."

"Are we there?" He spoke in a daze, sitting up in the seat and looking around. "Where are the people?"

"We are in Georgia," his mother said with a laugh.

"Oh…Is that close to Florida?"

"It's directly above it. On a map, y'know?"

"Yay!" Then he paused. "Why did we stop here?" He then looked to his left, out the window, and said, "Wow! Look at that! There is a camp."

"We are going to go check it out," Tanya replied. "So come on." She climbed out of the car.

The two children followed her closely. The campground in front of them was very exciting because although nobody said it at first, the same thought was going through the minds of all three people: there had to be people out there somewhere because the camp was new. There were faint tire tracks in the dirt, leading to the row of trucks. These tracks were fairly fresh, which could only mean people had been here recently.

Finally, Anna broke the silence, asking, "What do you think, Tanya?"

Tanya looked around one more time and laughed before responding. "I think this is excellent news. There are people out there somewhere, and I bet we will find them in Miami."

Anna asked, "They are gone though. Isn't that bad? Like, why did they leave?"

"To me, this looks like a temporary camp. Like it was set up for a short time as a base of operations or something, but that is just speculation on my part." Tanya looked down at the fire pit, which they had reached.

"Well, where is everybody? Did the creepers kill them?" This came from JR, who had been previously silent.

"No, the camp is way too prepared. It was left very organized, and there are no dead bodies around here." Tanya traced a circle in the dirt with her foot. "Honestly, it looks like whoever left it intends to return sometime."

Anna asked, "Then should we stay here and wait?"

After a brief contemplation, Tanya decided. "We are so close to Miami, we might as well just go there. I wouldn't be surprised if the people who built this camp went to Miami anyways."

Her reasoning seemed logical, so Anna asked, "Do you want to go look at the trucks?"

"I was just about to suggest that," Tanya said. "C'mon, JR." No response came. "JR?"

Both Tanya and Anna turned around to find the boy, who was pointing to the distant tree line. He suddenly shouted, "Creepers!"

Heads instantly snapped in the direction that he was pointing. The boy was right, and in the dying light, three creepers were visible sprinting toward the humans.

Anna, obviously caught off guard, asked Tanya, "Did you bring your gun?

"No, did you?"

"No." Tanya swore under her breath and asked, "What was I thinking?"

The beasts were closing the distance quickly. There was only one thing that they could do. Anna yelled out, "Run!"

The group of three all turned and began sprinting toward their car, which was about fifty yards away. The creepers were within earshot, snarling and growling as they chased their prey. JR was falling behind, so Tanya scooped him up and continued forward, running faster than she ever had in her life. They had come much too far to be killed here.

With the creepers bearing down on them from behind, they approached the car quickly. "We are not going to make it," Anna yelled.

Tanya, weighed down by JR, said, "No! We are going to be okay. Come on!"

The creepers were only twenty yards behind them, but the car was getting closer as well. Once they reached it, Anna sprinted around to the passenger's side while Tanya threw driver's door open. She sat JR down on the ground and yelled, "Jump in!"

The boy leapt into the car, landing in Anna's lap. "Come on, Mom," he yelled back at Tanya, and she also climbed in the car, slamming the door behind her. No sooner had the door closed when the three creepers hammered the side of the car, denting it with their brute force. It jolted violently, the force of the shock tilting it onto two wheels, and JR screamed in fear.

"Drive," Anna said. "Go!"

Tanya's only response was trying to shove the car keys in the ignition in the tilting car. She managed to say, "I'm trying!" Finally, the key found its mark, and with the twist of her wrist, the engine roared to life. One of the creepers lunged its hand through the driver's side window, completely shattering the glass. The pale hand groped toward Tanya, but she slapped it away and stepped on the gas.

The car lurched forward, and the creeper that had broken through the window grabbed on the frame of the car so that the beast was pulled along beside the vehicle, refusing to let go. The other creepers were left behind in a cloud of dust, but that did not stop them from sprinting after the car from behind with superhuman speed.

Tanya asked Anna, "Can you try to steer for me?" The girl nodded, and as she reached over to take the steering wheel, Tanya turned to the window and attempted to shake the creeper loose, but it refused to let go of the car frame.

The car had accelerated to thirty-five miles an hour, but still the monster clung on tightly with a grip of steel despite being violently dragged along the ground and constantly battered and cut by the terrain. Tanya fought to peel its fingers away from the frame, but she was nowhere near strong enough. She eventually asked, "JR, where is your hunting knife?"

"In the backseat."

"Can you get it for me?"

The car swerved violently around some debris in the road as JR set to work, climbing into the backseat and searching for his knife. After a few seconds, he finally found it and said, "It's right here, Mom!"

"Hand it to me, dear." She reached her hand out blindly in the backseat, and JR shoved the hilt of the knife into her palm. "Thanks," she panted as she swung the ten-inch blade at the creeper's wrist with as much force as she could muster.

There was a sickening sound as the knife blade dug bone-deep into the creeper's wrist. The beast bellowed out in pain and finally let go, disappearing behind them as the car drove on. "I hate those things," Anna said as Tanya once again began steering.

"I do too." She agreed. "There is no way that they can catch us in the car." She looked at the fuel gauge. "We need to stop and refill gas, but we can go another fifteen miles or so."

"We also need to check how badly the car is damaged too," added Anna, glancing at the shattered window beside Tanya.

"I agree."

Ten minutes later, they stopped in the middle of the road to refill the gas tank once they reached a clear area that seemed much less likely to have a creeper threat than the forest did. All three people got out of the car. Tanya opened the trunk and took out three more fuel cans, which she began emptying into the car's tank, while JR and Anna inspected the side of the car, which was dented violently.

CREEPERS 2

"Those creepers hit us hard," Anna said, tracing a large dent in the rear door on the driver's side with her fingers.

Tanya nodded but cracked a smile. "At least they didn't get to us. It will still drive."

JR asked, "How far are we from Miami?"

"Not nearly as far as when we started." Anna joked.

"If we drive through the night, we will easily be there by the morning," Tanya added. "Are you guys ready to go?"

Both JR and Anna answered, "Yeah!"

After another five minutes, everyone had loaded back into the car. They were soon headed through the darkness, searching for the hope, companionship, and humanity that they all believed was their final destination.

Tanya spoke everyone's thoughts, saying, "I believe there are people in Miami, I truly do, but I still can't help but think about that campsite. If only there had been people there, know what I mean?"

"Yes." Anna agreed. "I wonder where they all went." She looked out the window as the moon rose in the night sky, wondering where everyone had gone and what lay in store for her group—her family—in the near future.

10

Jason's legs were killing him. He swore that he had never been sitting down for as much time in his life as he had over the course of the last two days. The flight from the Australia colony to California had been horrible because of both its length and the constant view of nothing but ocean. The previous day, he had been so ready for a stretch by the time the plane had landed in California that he nearly jumped from his seat. After an uneventful night in San Francisco, he had boarded the plane again the next day and had been sitting in the cramped seat beside Michaela ever sense. Flying in a plane so soon was a horrible mixture of déjà vu and reoccurring claustrophobia.

"What's wrong?" Michaela was looking up at him. "You keep fidgeting."

"I'm fine! It's just that I need to stretch." He rubbed his legs.

She leaned to the right and peered out the window. The sun was hanging low in the evening sky, but it provided plenty enough light to see the earth below.

CREEPERS 2

"Well, you are in luck," Michaela said. "I see the camp down there."

She was correct. Only seconds later, Shade called out, "Fasten your seatbelts, ladies and gentlemen." The seatbelts clicked from all across the cabin, and the descent began. The runway being used was the same as before—a highway running adjacent to the camp that had been cleared by some of the men. It was makeshift, but it had worked just fine on the first mission.

As the plane dipped, the campsite came into view for Jason. From an aerial overlook, it appeared as something of an oval. The highway ran along the southern side. The "camp" itself was only a mere oval of short grass in the middle of a dense woodland area. Jason speculated that this area had been cleared for the construction of a shopping center of some sorts before the virus struck, but he would never be certain. In the very center of the oval was the rock and dirt fire pit the men had built. The tents would be assembled in rows nearby the fire as soon as they landed.

"It looks pretty cold out there," Michaela said. The trees were now completely bare, and crispy brown leaves were visible blowing across the camp in the light of the dying day. Jason took his gray jacket from his lap and dug out the gloves that he had shoved in the pockets, just in case. She mused, "I wonder how we will set up the camp."

Jason answered, "I'm not sure, but I bet Shade or Holder will tell us." He hadn't realized how close the plane had gotten to the ground, but seconds later, the cabin jumped slightly as the wheels made the initial contact. "Oh, wow." The plane thundered forward for several hundred yards down the empty highway where it eventually came to a stop.

The cabin had fallen quiet on the runway, but once the plane had finally stopped moving, the buzz of chatter began to build up. It grew insistently louder until Shade and Holder stood up in the front of the plane and began giving instructions.

Shade spoke first. "Thank you for your cooperation during the flight. I know that these trips can be both boring and tiresome." A general murmur of consensus followed, and he chuckled. "Still, there is no jetlag allowed. We have about an hour and fifteen minutes before the sun sets, and we need to get the tents set up and the supplies loaded into the trucks by then."

Holder continued, "So here is the plan, we are going to split into groups and get the tasks accomplished."

My men and I will take care of loading the trucks. You all need to follow me down to the hold, and we will start moving the crates to the trucks right out there." Shade pointed out the window to the row of six large trucks parked beside each other toward the edge of the camp. "Maxwell, follow us down to the hold, but you will get the duster and the welding equipment. I know you've been shown how to do everything, so weld it onto one of the helicopters. If you have any questions, it's fine to ask."

"Yes, sir," Maxwell called from the back of the cabin.

"Fantastic." Holder rubbed his hands together. "The rest of us will start by getting the tents and pitching them around the fire pit. We have sixteen, so some of us will have to share." He located Teddy and said, "Teddy, you should get the fire going and start dinner. We are all hungry." He smiled and put his hand on his stomach. "I can find you something to get the fire going if you come with me."

Shade asked, "Any questions?" None came, and he looked out the window again. "Also, remember that we aren't in Australia anymore. Creepers are here, and we might be immune to their virus, but that won't stop them from turning us into their meal." He nodded at Holder. "I should not be the one to explain this though. Holder has actually been here before and dealt with creepers in nature. I never have. Do you have any tips for if we encounter one of the monsters?"

Holder called out, "I think Jason and Michaela should be the ones to go over this. They have more experience than any of us when it comes to battling them. Come on up here, you two, and you can bring your gear."

Completely surprised by this, Jason and Michaela stood up and made their way to the front of the plane after taking their rifles from the overhead storage unit above them. Jason eyed Holder. "You just want us to talk about how to fight them?"

"Yes, just give us any tips that you have."

Jason turned to face the passengers and swallowed. He clutched the rifle in his hands tightly. "Well, creepers will almost always attack if they spot prey. That's just the way they are. They also always try to bite, so they make the majority of their attacks with their mouth. They obviously fight best at close range as well."

Michaela added, "But in the process of fighting them, never lose sight of how much we are like them. Creepers are just sick people, and never forget that. We have learned that killing a creeper is not too different than killing another man, so if a creeper is to attack, only try to injure it instead of killing it. That might be easier said than done because it is very easy to panic in a situation like that, but try to think before you pull the trigger. Remember every bullet carries a consequence."

Remembering another detail, Jason tossed in, "Creepers are also scared of fire up close, if that helps at all."

"Anything helps," said Holder. "Thank you both."

"It's no problem, honestly."

Holder now spoke to the entire group. "Daylight is falling fast, so let's get the move on! Let's get to work, ladies and gentlemen."

People rose to their feet, and one by one, they began to exit the plane. Jason and Michaela walked with Holder down to the storage hold, where they each grabbed a bag containing a tent. More of the people in Holder's group came and gathered similar tents working alongside Shade's men, who were beginning the daunting task of loading the crates into the supply trucks. Holder led his tent-bearing group toward the fire pit.

As they approached, he began saying, "With sixteen tents, let's make four rows of four and keep the fire pit centralized. Try to put at least twenty feet between the tents to keep them spaced out enough."

The group set to work. Jason and Michaela decided it would be easier to both work on one tent at a time, so they quickly set up the first large tent before advancing to the second. At that time, Teddy came wandering up to the fire pit wielding a cigarette lighter and rolling a wheeled ice chest behind him. He waved at the teens and held the lighter in the air. "I'm going to cheat in starting this fire. We have a ton of lighters in the supply crates, anyway."

Jason laughed at the big man and said, "Whatever gets us dinner fastest is best."

"I completely agree," answered Teddy. "We're having hamburgers tonight."

"Oh, that sounds really tasty, and you always do well." Michaela praised him as she helped Jason wrestle with one side of the tent.

Holder walked up to them as they finally got the tent to stand on its own. "Looks like both of you did a fine job."

"Thanks," answered Jason.

Holder watched Teddy coaxing the fire to life, and then he said, "Doesn't it feel kind of strange being back here so soon? We were here less than a week ago, but we've been halfway around the world twice since then."

"When you look at it that way, it does seem quite strange to be back," Michaela said.

Holder slowly turned and checked everyone's progress in assembling the tents. He decided, "We better help some of these folks."

He was right. Many of the people around them were struggling greatly in pitching their tents. For the next thirty minutes, the teenagers and Holder walked around and offered their assistance where it was needed. Michaela even ended up helping Teddy cook burgers over the large bonfire as Jason and Holder finished ensuring the rest of the tents were appropriately pitched.

Finally, the two of them walked over to Michaela and Teddy while the rest of the group stood around and talked about the mission, the camp, and everything in-between. Holder asked, "How is dinner coming, Teddy?"

Teddy nodded confidently. "I think I'm about done. Are all the tents good to go?" He quickly looked around the camp and said, "Never mind! I can answer that for myself."

Jason asked Holder, "Do you think Shade's men are about done?"

By now, the darkness was falling quickly, and Holder peered through it at the trucks about fifty yards away. "Yes, I think they are nearly finished. All of the trucks appear to be loaded." He then turned around and said, "And Maxwell must be done with the welding job. Here he comes now."

Maxwell approached the fire with his welding mask pulled to the top of his head. His long hair was matted with sweat. "The burgers smell excellent," he said. "And did I hear my name?"

"Yes," answered Holder. "We were just talking about how well Shade and his team are progressing."

"Oh, okay! I think that the rest of them are about done loading the supplies. I welded the duster onto a chopper, and I'm pleased with how it went."

"Fantastic, great job." Holder shook the man's hand. "We can eat as soon as the rest of the men are done loading the trucks."

Maxwell chuckled. "Then I hope they hurry up."

Suddenly, a scream rang out from the direction of the trucks. Jason could not identify who had yelled because the voice was distorted with terror. What he could understand, however, was the single word being called out, "Creeper!"

The camp burst into utter chaos. At least three people cried out or cursed in fear, not used to the threat of creepers. Across the camp, almost everyone seemed stunned, and they all froze in place. The only people to react to the outburst were the teenagers and Holder. As soon as the scream rang out, Jason reacted with blinding speed. He unstrapped his rifle from his back and took off in a dead sprint toward the direction it had come from. Michaela and Holder were right at his heels as he approached the group of Shade's men, who were all clustered around the edge of the dense tree line with guns raised.

"What happened?" Jason held his rifle high.

One of Shade's men tried to explain. "I saw a creeper watching us load the trucks. When it saw that I was looking, it ran into the trees." He seemed to fumble for the words.

"Get back from the tree line." Jason's voice was quiet but insistent, and the men did as the teenaged boy commanded them. After they had moved away from being dangerously close to the dark and dense forest, Jason crept forward with his rifle raised. Michaela and Holder still followed closely behind.

"Be careful." Shade instructed.

"Of course." Jason moved just into the trees and stood very still. He held his pointer finger up and tried to get the rest of the men silent. Once all of the noise had died down, the silence that followed grew omnipresent, white noise buzzing in his ears. Jason listened for almost an entire minute before stating, "If there was a creeper here, then it is not anymore."

Truman whispered, "How can you be sure?"

"I can just tell because I can't hear one. It's hard to explain." He stepped away from the trees. "Creepers have very heavy, wheezy breathing, and they are almost constantly growling. I've grown very good at recognizing the sounds. They are very distinct."

"He's right about that," said Michaela. "There is no creeper nearby. At least not anymore."

"If what you saw was actually a creeper," Jason began to say, "it must have fled very far away. That's a little unusual." He realized that he was sounding skeptical, so he added, "But that is still possible, creepers do some very unusual things."

Holder spoke up for the first time. "Well, regardless of what was seen, let's get back to the camp. Dinner is ready, so we can go eat, but we just need to be on high alert."

With that, the group turned from the dark forest and began heading back to the camp. On the way back, Shade asked, "Just in case that actually was a creeper, should we take turns having someone awake tonight to guard the camp?"

Holder considered the questions and answered, "I think that is a very good idea, Shade. I can even take the first watch."

"There is absolutely no way." Shade objected. "That was my idea, so I will take the first shift. I will watch until midnight, and Truman can go after me. If you insist, then you could go after him, Holder, but I believe we will be able to handle the job just fine. I slept on the plane all day anyway."

"Well, I will go after Truman," Holder declared. "But I want you to know that I am willing to do it first shift."

"Go ahead and rest up, then you can take over after me." Truman instructed, and it was hard to argue against such a large man.

"All right, fine. I'll be taking over at three o'clock tomorrow morning though," Holder informed as they were finally approaching the campfire. "Those burgers look so good."

The smell of hamburgers grew stronger, and Jason realized just how hungry he had become. The food completely drove the thought of creepers out of his mind, and he ate two burgers while spending the next hour socializing with the people on the rescue mission. Finally, as the moon was rising in the sky and darkness was falling all around them, Michaela asked, "Are you ready to go to sleep, Jason? I put our stuff in that tent." She pointed to a large tent beside him.

"Yeah, let me go tell Holder good night." Jason went and found Holder and told him that he and Michaela were going to sleep. He also added, "If you want me to help take a shift guarding the camp, let me know. I wouldn't mind at all."

Holder politely refused the offer and bid Jason a good night's rest, so he went back to the tent and lay down on a blanket beside Michaela. She was silent for a moment, but then questioned, "Well, are you excited to be in Miami tomorrow?"

"I'm so excited," Jason answered truthfully. "We will be one step closer to getting my brother back." For maybe the first time, he had confidence that the mission was going to be a success. Jason smiled and sank his head back into his pillow.

11

The drop in temperature was obvious, even inside the tent. Both Jason and Michaela were laying on a blanket folded in half over the hard ground. Even with the two blankets spread over the top of them and each other's body heat, the night seemed to be getting colder. They had been lying like this for over three hours now, but sleep evaded them both. They were not conversing, but his mind was still working hard trying to run through the plans for the next day. There was so much at stake on the mission, namely his brother's life, and still some of his questions seemed unanswered.

Jason took his arm and wrapped it around Michaela, pulling her against him for warmth. He rubbed his hand up and down her side gently but stopped when she whispered, "I can't sleep. I'm thinking too much about tomorrow."

"Me too."

Outside, the sound of footsteps crunched by in the dead grass. A shadow, cast from the campfire, flickered across the side of the tent. It was the silhouette of Truman, recognizable by the mass and the dreadlocks that bounced up and down as the man walked. He was clutching a rifle, patrolling the tents while on the lookout for the creeper that managed to evade the group earlier. Jason felt relieved knowing that someone was actually guarding the camp while he slept—a feeling completely new to him. The sound of the footsteps grew fainter until they could not be heard at all.

"We probably need some rest." Michaela admitted. She turned to Jason. "Will you try to relax and catch a few hours of sleep? It's actually kind of peaceful out here if you think about it." She paused for a brief moment and then said, "Just close your eyes and listen to the insects in the forest. I bet that didn't happen much in New York."

Jason smiled at this. "When we get Drake back, I'll ask him."

"Good night, Jase."

"Good night, Michaela."

Jason closed his eyes again, attempting to relax his brain and become sleepy. Michaela was right, the sound of insects gently echoed from all around. He slowly began drifting to sleep while telling himself that soon his brother was going to be back. Slowly his brain seemed to be shutting down, relaxing, and embracing rest.

Jason was with Michaela sitting at a table and playing cards. They sat at a green table that was well lit by an unseen light, but the rest of the room surrounding the table was almost completely black. Michaela studied her hand in the card game and asked, "Do you have any twos?"

Jason rifled through his handful of cards and said, "Go fish."

His girlfriend took a card from the top of a pile setting on the table between them, but they soon were interrupted when the sound of approaching footsteps came from the far side of the room. They drew nearer until a recognizable person emerged into the light surrounding the table.

Jason and Michaela both exclaimed, "Drake!"

In the dream, Jason's younger brother looked the same as he always had. He had the same messy-yet-maintained dark hair, warm eyes, and cocky smile that sometimes was scarily similar to Jason's own. He was wearing a red T-shirt and jeans; a rifle was draped over his shoulder. Drake looked at Michaela first and then his brother. "What's up, guys?"

Jason walked around the table and embraced his brother. "I missed you. I'm so glad you are back."

Drake put his hand on Jason's back and patted it, replying, "I'm glad you missed me, but technically, I'm not back yet."

"What do you mean?"

Drake laughed. "You do realize that you are dreaming, right?"

"Oh, yeah." Jason admitted. "But we are coming to get you back, I promise! We are going to get you tomorrow. Everything is planned out."

Drake smiled. "That is exciting." He looked at his wrist for the time, which was strange considering he wasn't wearing a watch. The boy declared, "I better get going for now. See you later!"

Neither Jason nor Michaela had the chance to say good-bye before Drake disappeared in an overly dramatic flash of smoke. The smoke hadn't even cleared before the sound of footsteps came from the darkness on the other side of the table. The steps drew nearer until yet another recognizable figure stepped up to the table. It was a middle-aged man wearing dark clothes and with a rugged-looking beard and untamed hair. He spoke. "Hello, Jason."

"Fox?" Jason immediately recognized the wild-looking man. Fox had helped Jason and Drake escape New York City on the way to the Miami settlement. He had saved both of the brothers' lives on multiple occasions, even going as far as to sacrifice his own life for theirs.

Fox laughed at Jason's surprised expression. "What's the matter? You look like you've seen a ghost."

Jason stammered. "You…you died saving our lives."

Fox casually dusted some dirt off of his worn leather jacket and replied, "You're welcome, by the way." He laughed again and then looked at Michaela. "And what is this? Have you got you a girl?" Extending his hand across the table to Michaela, he greeted, "I'm Fox."

Michaela smiled and sincerely replied, "I have heard so much about you, and it is great to finally meet you." She paused and then tossed in, "And I'm Michaela, sorry!"

"You're fine, dear." Fox sat down at the table and turned to Jason. "I never had the opportunity to say good-bye, Jason. You were a great friend to me, and I enjoyed our time together. Thank you."

A shout came from the distance, but it was still distinguishably Drake's voice. "Hey, Fox, we better go! Our time is up. Jason needs to survive if he is going to save me, and you can't keep him too long."

Jason was sad to think about losing Fox, and he blinked back a tear. "You saved both me and my brother's lives several times, and you were kind of like a father to us. It should be me thanking you instead."

"You're right," Fox said as he stood. "What was I thinking? Sorry, Jason, but you and your girl better get going before the fight gets too bad." He stood and began walking away, unlike Drake, who had simply disappeared.

Now Jason was confused. "What are you talking about? What fight? Survive what? I'm only asleep!" He looked to Fox, but the man had faded into the darkness.

Michaela spoke, taking him by surprise. "Jason, can you not hear the gunshots?"

"Gunshots?"

"Listen, Jason!" She stood up and began walking around the table.

As he listened more closely, Jason realized that he did, in fact, hear gunshots. They were distant, but still obvious. "Michaela, what is going on?"

Michaela pointed to the chair Jason was sitting in. "Get up, Jason."

He was so confused. "No! I'm still tired!"

Michaela suddenly grabbed Jason and began trying to tug him out of the chair. She was yelling now, "Jason! Get up! Get up, Jason! You've got to get up!"

"What's going on? Where are the gunshots coming from?"

"Just get up, Jason!" She shook him by the collar of his shirt, trying to get him out of the chair and onto his feet. "Get up, Jason!"

"Get up, Jason!" Jason's eye's snapped open. Michaela was sitting on him and shaking him violently.

"Why? What's going on?"

Jason was sitting up when a gunshot rang out into the dark night. Michaela swore and said, "Those shots are getting closer."

He rolled Michaela to the side and grabbed his rifle. She was already clutching hers. "What is going on?"

"It's the creepers! They must have made it to the camp. From the sounds of things, I'd say they already killed three of our men at least." Michaela was talking extremely fast and shaking. "Jason, I thought we were done with this!"

More gunshots pierced the night. The unmistakable yell of Truman thundered out, "I got one!" He sounded nearby the teenager's tents.

Another voice yelled out to Truman, "What's going on? I'm here to help!"

Inside the tent, Jason looked to Michaela. "That was Teddy's voice. Let's go see if we can help."

Both of the teenagers checked to make sure their rifles were loaded and ready to fire. They both had the maximum rounds loaded, which was always vital no matter how many creepers were attacking. "Let's go," Jason whispered, and the two slipped out of the tent.

Outside, things were dark, but a full moon hanging in the sky provided enough light to discern what was occurring. Ten yards to Jason's left, the round frame of Teddy, red-faced and wheezing, came lumbering forward. Another twenty yards in the opposite direction, Truman stood in front of another tent in the same row.

Teddy coughed and asked, "Did you kill all of them creepers? I don't see any."

Truman, pistol in hand, whirled around and faced Teddy. He bit his lower lip in contemplation with a dangerous look on his face, and he opened his mouth as if he was going to say something, but then he closed it and froze. Finally, he managed to say, "Just know that this is nothing against the burgers." With that, he raised the pistol and fired. As Jason watched in horror, two bullets slammed into Teddy's chest, and the large man was thrown off his feet and onto the ground with a fountain of blood spewing from the wounds.

Jason was completely terrified and confused. He looked to Michaela, who also looked completely perplexed, and then he looked back to Truman. The massive black man seemed to spot the teenagers for the first time now, stepping backward in surprise. He took a deep breath and lifted his pistol again, aiming it at them.

For the first time in his life, Jason was staring down the barrel of a gun. "Get down!" He grabbed Michaela and threw her to the ground, reacting with amazing speed as he dove down beside her. Shots were fired, and three holes were torn in Jason's tent only a split-second later. Truman aimed the pistol again and fired at Jason, who frantically rolled to the side as the bullets threw dirt into the air right where he had been. The massive man swore as Jason managed to get a grip on his own rifle and returned a volley of bullets. Truman reeled back from the shots, and Jason yelled to Michaela, "Run!"

She pushed herself out of the dirt and took off into the night. Jason followed directly behind her. By this time, Truman had managed to regain his composure, and he took shots at the teenagers as they sprinted away. The bullets came dangerously close—Jason swore that he felt one buzz by his neck—but none of them made contact with either him or Michaela.

Still confused about what was happening but aware of the present threat, Michaela pointed her rifle behind her as she sprinted away. The gun unleashed a chain of fire at their attacker. None of the shots landed where they were intended, but they did give the teenagers enough time to dive behind another tent and hide from Truman.

Enraged by the escape, Truman bellowed into the night. More gunfire chattered from across the camp and the sound of a woman screaming in pain followed. Jason peered around his cover and tried to distinguish what was going on. He decided the latest gunshots hadn't come from Truman, who was slowly looking around and trying to spot the teenagers in the dark night.

A new voice came from nearby Truman, a voice both Jason and Michaela recognized. "What happened? Did something go wrong?"

"The kids got away." Truman sounded furious.

"You better be joking." The second voice also demonstrated anger, but it was more controlled than Truman's. "How could you lose two teenagers?" The unmistakable figure of Shade emerged from the darkness behind Truman. He was clutching a pistol and had an AK-47 strapped on his back. He spoke in a demanding way. "Find them. Kill them. None of the others can live, even if they are just kids."

At this point, two more men walked up to the scene. Jason recognized them as some of Shade's men, but he didn't know either of their names. One man was broad and muscular, while the other man was slim and short. Both were gripping rifles, and the short man appeared to have blood on his pants.

Shade asked, "Can I get a status update?"

The short man said, "We have taken care of our list. Clinton and Maxwell are done with theirs, too. How has it gone for you?"

Shade said, "Truman let the stupid teenagers get away for now, but he killed both Teddy and Holder."

There was a pause, and then Truman told Shade, "I thought that you had Holder?"

Shade contemplated the question and then asked, "You mean you didn't kill him?"

"No, I thought that was your job." Truman dropped his gaze to the ground.

Shade completely snapped, swearing relentlessly into the darkness. He then became furious and started yelling, a side that the teenagers had never seen from the brilliant man. "Killing Holder was your job! Are you telling me that he is still out there?" Truman didn't respond, so Shade turned to the other two men. "Did either of you kill him?"

"No."

Shade swore and then cupped his hands over his mouth and yelled to the rest of his men across the camp. "Holder and the kids are still out there. I want them found and killed. Now!"

The group dispersed and began to search throughout the camp. Michaela grabbed Jason's arm. "What on earth is going on?"

He shook his head. "I have no idea, but we can't stick around to find out. We have to go." Rifle in hand, Jason stood to a crouched position and crept into the darkness before him. He whispered, "Come on."

Michaela followed Jason through the camp, but finding no apparent place to hide, they continued forward from tent to tent, using them as cover from sight. Meanwhile, the sound of footsteps was growing persistently closer. Truman's voice thundered out, "Where are you, children? Come out, come out!"

After diving behind another tent with Jason, Michaela quietly asked, "Should we shoot Truman? He's not too far away."

Jason, still trying to figure out what to do, replied, "No, we might kill him, but there are far more of them than there are of us. If we turn this into a gunfight, we will lose for sure."

The sound of heavy footfall was only yards away when Jason heard something. He looked at Michaela. "Was that you?"

"What?"

"Did you whistle?"

She shook her head. Nearby, Truman called out, "If you surrender now, then we might not even kill you. We can talk options." He was only yards away, mere seconds from spotting the teenagers.

In the silence, Jason heard the whistle again. This time, he figured out where it was coming from. In a flash, he grabbed Michaela, and they both dove into the tent they had been hiding behind right as Truman walked by. The enormous man paused, looked around, and then continued forward past their hiding place.

Jason and Michaela were greeted by the dark and shadowy figure of Holder kneeling inside the tent with a pistol in one hand and a grenade in the other. He whispered, "I'm glad that you heard me, Jason."

Not wasting any more time, Jason feverishly whispered, "What on earth is happening out there?"

In the darkness inside the tent, he barely managed to make out the shape of Holder shaking his head. The man answered, "I'm not even sure. For some reason, Shade's men have gone rogue and killed everyone. I never suspected anything, and they blindsided us in the night."

Michaela, beginning to piece things together, breathed, "That must be why Shade insisted on having the watch shift."

"You are right." Jason agreed. "But what are we going to do?" He looked to Holder with his question.

The military-minded man considered the situation and was about to answer when a voice from across the camp yelled out, "I can't find any of them! They must be hiding inside the tents."

Holder cursed but was drowned out as Truman bellowed, "Check inside the tents. They have got to be in one of them." Instinctively, Holder and the teenagers gripped their weapons even tighter.

The voice of Shade commandingly rang out across the camp. "No, don't approach the tents. As stupid as all of you can be, I still can't afford to lose any of you. Keep in mind that all three of the runaways are armed, so if you open a tent with one of them inside, thirty rounds will be pumped into your chest before you blink."

Truman sounded confused. "What are we supposed to do, boss?"

"This." From inside the tent, Jason could not see what was going on outside, but the sounds that followed told the story. A lengthy chatter of gunfire came, and the sound of a different tent being torn to complete threads was audible.

Truman pressed. "You want us to shoot the tents? *Our* tents?"

"Yes!" Shade's tone suggested there was little room for argument. "We have more anyway. Shoot the tents right now! I want them to be completely obliterated!"

There was a brief moment of eerie silence—the calm before the storm. Holder looked to Jason and Michaela. He looked scared, which was an emotion that his face rarely showed. Still, he fought it back and yelled out, "Run!"

From all around, gunshots tore into the night. They came from seemingly every direction as Jason,

Michaela, and Holder all leapt out of the tent where they had been hiding. Only a split second later, a wall of bullets tore it down. Someone across the camp yelled, "There they are! All three of them are together!" More gunfire came their way.

Holder proved impressively fast, getting out ahead of both Jason and Michaela. Jason struggled to get his footing in the loose dirt and dead grass, and for a split second, he thought he was going to fall, but he managed to regain his balance. He had faced many dangers in his life, but being shot at was a first. Holder seemed to be purposefully running, so Jason yelled, "Where are we going?" He struggled to make himself heard over the gunfire coming from behind them, sending a spray of bullets their direction.

Mid-sprint, Holder hollered back, "The supply trucks are dead ahead. The keys are even in the ignition. If we can get there, we might get away."

Apparently, Shade heard this because from behind them, he yelled, "Don't let them reach the trucks. After them!"

He was too late. The group of three continued the dead sprint, wind whipping in their ears, across the flat ground until the supply trucks were visible in the darkness ahead. These trucks, pickups with supply crates loaded in the back, were various colors but about the same size. Holder seemed to be targeting a white one, and he was the first one to reach it. He threw the driver's side door open, jumped inside, and turned the key that was already in the ignition. The truck roared to life.

A torrent of swearing came from behind Jason and Michaela as they ran to the passenger's side. Michaela threw the door open and climbed inside as Jason returned fire on Shade's men. Once she was in, he leapt into the cab of the truck while slamming the door shut in one fluid motion. He had barely made contact with the seat before the large truck lurched forward. Holder turned the truck violently to the right to dodge a few stray bullets, and after driving straight for fifty yards, he turned right again onto the road that was being used as a runway. The three had miraculously escaped unscathed from the midnight bloodbath, and the truck carried them deeper into the night.

12

Shade watched the white truck drive away. He was so furious that he was struggling to maintain his composure. It was mere seconds later when another one of the supply trucks roared to life. Two of his men, Maxwell and a short and slim man named Douglass, had climbed into another one of the trucks, and it sped forward in pursuit of the escapees. From across the camp, Shade called out, "Don't come back until they are dead." The truck turned and drove out of sight. He watched it disappear, shaking his head. He turned to Truman and asked, "How could something go this wrong? They were supposed to be killed in their sleep."

Truman consoled. "Don't worry, boss. Maxwell will see to it that they are dead."

"He better." Shade kicked the ground in anger. "We can't afford to risk them ruining our plans."

"What should we do while we wait?" This came from Clinton, a bald man whose mouth seemed to form a permanent scowl.

Shade paced around for a brief moment, pondering, and then he finally concluded. "The show still goes on."

He turned to Truman. "We will wait about an hour for Maxwell and Douglass to return, but if they aren't back by then, we will set out to Miami. The mission can succeed without Douglass, and Maxwell already did his job, so we don't need him anymore either. We can't afford for Holder and the kids to come back and try to pick a fight if they somehow kill our men."

"This will be very hard to pull off with just six." Truman acknowledged.

Shade spit back, "You think I don't know that? What do we do, go back to Australia with five men? That would arouse way too many questions. Keep in mind there won't be only six of us for long."

"Oh, yeah," Truman answered. He then asked, "When will help arrive?"

"Tomorrow, assuming we can last that long." Shade's voice seemed a little more level now, but the anger in it was far from discreet.

"Don't worry about it too much," Clinton said. "I'm sure Maxwell and Douglass can handle Holder and two kids."

"It seems we have no choice but to find out."

By driving across the dangerous and decrepit roads, it was soon obvious that they had not been driven on for years. They were littered with trash and environmental debris like tree branches. Nevertheless, Holder seemed to keep the gas pedal to the floor, and the truck accelerated and progressively gained speed. The ride was bumpy, but still the distance between the escapees and the pursuers stayed about the same. In the cab of the white truck, Jason asked, "What are we going to do?"

"I'm really not sure," Holder answered. "Hold on." He swerved the truck around a fallen tree branch. "Do either of you have any ideas?"

After looking out the rear window at the pursuers, Michaela asked, "Is there any chance that we can outrun them?"

Holder shook his head. "I doubt it. They can go just as fast as we can."

Jason peered out of the back window. "I'm not trying to be the bearer of bad news, but they are gaining ground on us."

Holder swore and then said, "I'm doing everything that I can. We can't risk going much faster, or we will wreck for sure. The road has too much debris on it." The timing couldn't have been any more coincidental, for as soon as he said that, Holder pointed out the front windshield. "What is that?"

A large and dark object sat in the middle of the road, obscuring the pathway. Michaela squinted into the darkness and replied, "I think that is a rock."

Only twenty yards away now, the object came in plain sight: a small boulder was in the middle of the highway. Holder asked, "How did that even get there?". Shaking his head, he instructed, "Hold on!" He seized the steering wheel with one hand and swung it to the right aggressively. The entire truck lurched to the side and skidded across the road so sharply that sparks were cast into the night sky. The pursuing truck now anticipated what was coming, so it moved farther to the right side of the road and avoided the boulder without any problem. "Now they are even closer." Holder shook his head. The situation certainly wasn't looking favorable for any of them. "Could this get any worse?"

The chatter of gunfire rang out from behind them. Jason shouted, "He has an AK." Suddenly, the rear windshield of their truck shattered into a spider web of cracks as two bullets pierced it before burying themselves in the cab's ceiling. Neither Holder nor the teenagers were harmed, the situation was looking even grimmer.

As the barrage of shots continued, Holder weaved the truck back and forth on the road to avoid gunfire. The maneuver worked temporarily, but Jason said, "We can't keep this up forever."

Holder yelled over the gunfire, "Well, do you have any ideas?"

Spotting a road leading to the right, Michaela burst out, "Turn there!"

Holder did as instructed, making the dangerously sharp turn which led to more skidding. The truck fishtailed, but it soon righted itself and began gaining speed. For a moment, the gunfire ceased. Seconds later, the pursuing truck rounded the same corner and was once again following closely. The gunfire continued as rounds drilled into the tailgate.

"We have to duck!" Holder dipped his head just low enough to see over the dashboard as he drove. Jason and Michaela did the same just in time as several more bullets burst through the truck's rear window. They tore through the cabin and smashed through the front windshield as well, cracking it so much that visibility was completely lost.

"That's not good," cried Jason.

"I can't see at all!" Holder tried to peer through the front windshield, but his view was completely obscured.

Jason could feel the truck swerving side to side down the road, but there was nothing that could be done about it. Holder was slowing the truck down, knowing that he couldn't continue to drive with the window in this condition. "I guess that it is over now," Jason mumbled.

"Yeah, I don't think we can—"

Holder's response was completely cut off when the truck slammed into an unseen object in the middle of the road. There was a horrible sound of tearing metal, and a weightless feeling overtook the cabin. Everyone screamed as the airborne truck began to spiral through the air. Michaela grabbed onto Jason as the truck began falling to the ground. It landed on its right side, ripping off the side mirror immediately and crunching the passenger's door inward. After skidding across the ground for almost sixty feet, the wrecked truck came to a complete rest.

The air bag had deployed, so Michaela shoved it out of her face and asked, "Are both of you okay?"

Holder was the first to respond. "I'm alive. I don't think I hurt anything. Jason?"

Jason sounded pained. "The door cut my arm, but it's not too bad."

"Let me be the judge of that." Michaela demanded as she grabbed Jason's hand. He tried to pull away and hide his injury, but she refused to let him succeed. Upon studying his hand, she gasped. "This is horrible." The sharp and jagged metal of the truck's caved-in door had left a deep gash in Jason's forearm that was almost four inches long. The wound was bleeding profusely.

Holder inspected too. "Oh no, you need to apply some pressure."

"Okay." Michaela was already peeling off her shirt. "Give me your arm."

Jason reluctantly raised his arm so that she could reach it, and she tied her shirt tightly against the bleeding wound. He objected. "It's way too cold for that! You need a shirt."

She dismissed it. "It doesn't matter if we don't get out of the situation anyway."

"If that is your argument, then why are you even trying to help?"

"Shade's men are getting closer," Holder whispered. "I'm going to try to take care of them."

Jason, teeth clenched in pain, managed to say, "That's suicide! Let us help you."

Holder shook his head. "You are not in any condition to fight, and I have another idea."

"What are you going to do?" Michaela sounded worried.

Holder reached up to the driver's side door, which was directly above him. His only response was, "I'm completely trusting that you both can stay in here and be silent for now." He looked to Michaela. "Have your rifle ready, and when I use the word 'Miami,' then you open fire on them." He pushed the door open overhead.

Jason said, "No!" Holder, however, only looked at Jason and put his finger over his lips. He then took a deep breath and began climbing out of the truck.

One of Shade's men commanded. "Don't move."

Holder, now with his torso out of the truck, tossed his pistol to the road and said, "It's over. You win." He sniffled as if he had been crying. "You killed my friends. Seriously, how can you live with yourselves? Killing your peers is wrong, but two teenagers… That's a whole new level." He paused, sniffled again, and then climbed out of the truck. "I can't believe this. I was so close to those two, but now…" His voice trailed off. "Michaela broke her neck. Jason took a bullet. I hope you truly realize what you have done." Holder's acting job was phenomenal, and he sounded very convincing.

Inside the truck, Michaela looked at Jason and whispered, "He's good." Jason nodded slightly.

Holder took another step toward the men, saying, "I surrender. I don't know what all of you are doing, but I can help. Take me to Shade." In the road between them was the trunk of a fallen tree, which Holder assumed is what caused the wreck.

Maxwell, who had been driving the pursuing truck, looked to the other man, Douglass. "What do we do? Since the teenagers are dead, would boss want Holder?"

"Come on, guys, I can help you." Holder persisted.

Douglass asked, "How do we know that you aren't lying to us?"

Holder faltered briefly, but he managed to come up with something. "Survival is important to me, and if you are to hop in your truck and drive off without me, then I will end up dying out here in the woods by myself. I'd have absolutely no chance."

Maxwell looked skeptically at Douglass. "Come here. We will bind your wrists so you aren't able to try anything."

"If that's what it takes, go for it." Holder slowly advanced toward them, arms outstretched. "I don't know why you are having problems trusting me, though, when I have never deceived either of you in my life. It was you, on the other hand, that just killed the majority of the campers—my friends."

Douglass pointed his rifle at Holder. "Watch it. Don't go there. We only did what we had to do."

In the wrecked truck, Michaela was clutching her rifle and ready to attack in a moment's notice. She was completely prepared when Holder said, "Sorry, I truly am." He forced a smile. "It's becoming obvious that I'm not too sure what is going on with the mission anymore, but I think I will be good assistance in helping you all cure Miami, if that is even still the plan."

Hearing the code word, Michaela sprang into action. While Holder was talking, she had moved so that one foot rested on the driver's seat and the other on the steering wheel before stretching out of the open driver's side door above her head and opening fire on the unprepared men. Several rounds of bullets sank into Douglass's chest, and he instantly dropped to the street. Maxwell, on the other hand, responded much more quickly to the surprise assault. He dove backward behind the other truck and returned a round of bullets back at Michaela, who ducked down into the cabin.

CREEPERS 2

Holder, surprised by Maxwell's speedy reaction, saw his opportunity and made a break for the pistol that he had thrown down on the street. He grabbed it, whirled around to face Maxwell, and pulled the trigger twice. Both shots missed to the right. Now Maxwell leaned out from behind his cover and shot back at Holder. The only difference was that he didn't miss like Holder had. One of the bullets struck Holder, and the man yelled out in pain before collapsing to the street.

Michaela watched in horror. She screamed, "You shot him!" Acting in a fury, she leapt out of the truck and dropped to the ground. She shot toward Maxwell several times, but he remained behind his cover.

His reply came. "Holder lied to me. He said you were dead." Maxwell fired at Michaela, but she dove behind the wrecked truck.

"Well, he was wrong. I'm not dead."

"Not yet." More bullets came in her direction, but most of them only slammed into the upturned truck, while the rest disappeared into the tree line. Michaela took aim once again and pulled the trigger of her assault rifle, but the only response was a dreaded clicking sound. She tried it again but had the same result. From across the road, the sound of laughter came from where Douglass had been hiding. He stood up and said, "Sounds like you are out of bullets, little girl." The man, gun raised, began advancing forward.

Michaela panicked. He was only a few feet away by the time she managed to say, "Please… no." Her voice sounded weak and frail.

Maxwell ran his eyes up and down over Michaela. "What is this?" He smiled sinisterly. "Decided to strip for me, did you? Isn't it a little cold to go without a shirt?" He kept coming.

Michaela, angered by his crude remarks, shouted, "Don't even look at me!"

"You can't do anything about it, little girl." He seized Michaela by the wrists. "You are actually quite attractive...for a runaway. Come here, we're going to have a little fun."

"Don't touch me!" She kicked out, but the man was much stronger than she was, and the effort was futile.

Maxwell laughed again. "I can do whatever I want to. Who is going to stop me?"

The reply came in the form of a gunshot. A bullet slammed into Maxwell's temple and killed him instantly, blood spraying from the hole in his skull. His lifeless body dropped to the street. Michaela turned to locate the shooter and beamed when she saw Jason, who had managed to climb out of the truck and jump down to the street. He was holding a rifle with a look of hatred on his face. "Nobody touches my girl."

Michaela ran to him and threw her hands around him. "Thank you, Jason. I was so scared that you couldn't climb out of the truck 'cause of your arm."

"It was kind of a challenge, but I certainly wasn't going to leave you out here alone."

Michaela pulled away from his embrace and said, "Let me see your arm."

"No." Jason shook his head. "We need to check on Holder first. Is he dead?"

From across the street, Holder's voice mumbled, "I can't believe you seriously just asked that." He laughed. "Where is your confidence in the old man?"

Jason turned to see Holder, who was still on the ground, but sitting up. He and Michaela ran to their fallen friend, checking on him. Jason asked, "What happened?"

Holder had rolled up the leg of his pants, inspecting his right shin. There was a bullet hole that was oozing blood. "He shot me in the leg. I might have blacked out for a second from hitting my head when I fell." He wiped the blood off and inspected the wound further. "Missed my shinbone, however. If I can get some pressure on it and slow the bleeding, I will be better off. It's really not that bad."

He looked at Jason and then Michaela. She was shivering with her arms crossed for warmth. "Talk to Jason about getting my shirt."

Holder shook his head. "No, go to the truck over there." He pointed to the truck that had been pursuing them. "Look in the back and see if there is another supply crate. It should be obvious and marked with a red cross."

While Michaela was going to the truck to look for supplies, Jason knelt down and used his good arm to study the wound. "The bullet passed all the way through."

"I guess I'm lucky that it didn't hit any arteries." Holder smiled.

With her arms full of gauze, bandages, and hydrogen peroxide, Michaela returned to Holder. She set the supplies down beside Jason and said, "Start working on the wound. I saw some clothes in a crate back there, and I'm going to go get a shirt before I get hypothermia. It's way too cold out here."

She left, and Jason did as instructed. He poured the peroxide in the wound and used his good arm to tightly wrap gauze around it and then bandages around that. Five minutes later, he finished. "How does that feel?"

Holder nodded. "The pressure is helping." Blood had not soaked through the bandage yet, so that was a good sign.

"Can you walk?"

The tree trunk that had caused the wreck was behind Holder. He turned around and snapped a dead branch off and used it to help him get onto his feet. Using his makeshift walking stick, he limped all the way to the truck where Michaela had finished changing. She looked at him, impressed, and said, "Well, you are getting along well."

Holder nodded. "I've been shot worse than this." Finally at the truck, he began digging through the medical supplies and took out a needle and suture. "Come here, Jason."

Jason held up his hands in objection. "No, I'm fine. I swear!"

The resistance did no good. It took several minutes of sitting on the truck's tailgate, but Holder managed to sterilize and stitch the gash in Jason's arm shut. He smiled at his completed work and then said, "We need to talk about this."

"My injury?"

"No, Shade." Holder looked at the ground. "I should have seen this coming, but I didn't, and now we are in danger because of it."

Jason was confused. "You knew Shade was going to do this?"

"No. Not at all." Holder looked to the cloudless night sky above the group. "But I think I know what he is doing, and we have to stop him. If he's doing what I think he might be up to, then this is really, really bad news." He stood and began limping to the truck's cabin. "I'm not in any condition to drive, but we really need to get back to the camp and try to stop Shade."

Jason wrapped the shirt around his stitched arm again and said, "I'll drive. I have a couple times before. You have to explain what's going on as we go."

As he climbed into the truck on the passenger's side, Holder said, "I can do that. Now gather your weapons, reload your gun, Michaela, and let's go. We can't waste any time."

13

Jason had forgotten a few of the basic skills of driving, but it soon came back to him with Holder coaching as they went. With instruction, he managed to turn the truck around without crashing into the tree trunk that had caused Holder to wreck, and then they set off back in the direction from which they had come. Throughout the entire chase, they had only turned once, so retracing the path should not be too difficult.

Once they were back on the correct route to the camp, Jason said, "Okay, Holder. Tell us why Shade decided to murder all of the campers and take over the mission."

"That's a tough one." Holder shook his head.

The truck bounced as it hit a pothole, and Holder winced. "Sorry." Jason apologized and then asked, "What do you mean?" He wanted to look at the man but refrained because he was driving.

"I guess that I should start with a history lesson for you two." Holder looked out the window and said, "I'm not even sure where I should begin." He paused and then continued, "Shade is power-hungry. He always has been."

Michaela asked, "What do you mean?"

"When we voted for leader of the Australian society, it turned into a very close race between Shade and Gordon," Holder started. "And to the public eye, the two seemed to be friends. They still do."

Jason cautiously drove around the boulder that they had almost crashed into during the chase, and then he asked, "But I'm guessing they weren't best friends?"

"No." Holder shook his head. "Gordon trusted Shade completely, and after a while, Shade gained my trust. He has always been different, and I just thought it was because of his intellect. Do you know what I mean? Like how actors were sometimes kind of strange people because of their career."

"Yeah, that makes sense, but go on." Michaela prompted.

"Okay. Being someone who was on the inside and close to both of them, I could tell that Shade wasn't happy with how the election went. He felt like he deserved the position more than Gordon, and I hate to say this, but he was probably right. Honestly, Shade is a better leader, and he is smarter, too. Being the one to have founded the colony, however, Gordon was viewed as the savior of the world. He won the vote based on what he had done in the past as opposed to what he would do in the future."

Jason nodded. "I can understand Shade being somewhat upset with how the election went, but how does that lead to his mass murder?" He stepped on the brake as something moved in the tree line, but nothing appeared so he proceeded forward.

Holder felt his leg again, presumably to see if the gunshot wound was still bleeding. After a pause, he continued, "Shade seemed happy enough when Gordon named him second-in-command, which was a great decision by Gordon because Shade has since showed how fantastic he is at decision-making. He also had great leadership skills and proved to be very talented at organizing things."

"What do you mean?"

"Well, remember what I told you about the cure? Shade was the one who worked with the doctors to create it, and it came from his ideas. The cure is Shade's baby, and he did many other things to prepare for this rescue mission."

The camp was beginning to appear in the distance, looming out of the darkness because of the large campfire. Jason said, "If this mission was so important to Shade, then why did he go and ruin everything?"

"This is the part where the power comes into play," Holder said. "I'm beginning to think a rescue mission wasn't Shade's intention, even from day one."

"What do you mean? Why would he even come here then?"

"Gordon told me that Shade helped plan the rescue mission while I was still in America with you two. The mission was going to happen anyway, but having your brother left in America only sped things up even more, Jason." Holder took a second to collect his thoughts. "Gordon also said that Shade was the one who selected the people who were going on this mission, which explains why there are so many of his new 'friends.'"

"So you think this was all premeditated." Michaela disgustedly shook her head. "I guess I am beginning to see where this is going."

"Yes, Shade and the rest of his men must have planned everything out a long time ago, maybe even months. Just before I left on the rescue mission to the Americas, he was beginning to go see some of his friends quite often, or, at least, that is what he told me. In hindsight, I'm wondering if he was planning out all of this."

"I remember when we first met him," Jason said, "he left because he had to go to a meeting. I bet you are right, Holder. All of this was probably planned for a very, very long time. We just somehow managed to get stuck in the middle of it."

"The big question is what exactly is his plan?" This came from Michaela.

The camp was even closer as Holder concluded. "I could be wrong, but I'm guessing that Shade and his men are going to go to Miami and attempting to cure the creepers there."

"What good would that do? That was the original plan all along," Jason said as he turned off the truck's headlights so it wouldn't be spotted by Shade and his men.

Michaela exclaimed, "Wait, I think I get it! Shade is attempting to start his own society, but here in America! He has the cure, and now all he needs is the citizens. He's going to drop the cure, and he and his men will start over again—a new beginning."

"I'm only wondering what Shade plans to do once he has founded a colony. What will happen when he has command over a bunch of people that he saved?" Holder sounded very worried. "What if he uses his influence to convince his people to attack the Australian colony, just for revenge? Or even for resources maybe? God knows those are scarce."

"That is exactly why we have to stop this right now. We can't let Shade pull this off. There are five of them now and three of us." Jason parked the truck. They were only three hundred yards from the camp now. The campfire seemed to be burning higher than ever before, and a quick scan of the campground revealed no movement. "I don't see Shade or any of the other men. Do you think they've left?"

"There is only one way to find out." Holder opened the door of the truck and grabbed his pistol.

Jason held up his hand to stop Holder. "No!" He sounded adamant. "You can barely walk, Holder, so you aren't going. You need to stay in the truck."

"I can't let you to go out there on your own against Shade and his armed men. You are just kids."

Michaela couldn't help but laugh. "Yet we were the only two Americans to survive the virus. I promise we can take care of ourselves. Stay here, Holder."

He sighed. "Unfortunately, I know you are right." He then said, "At least, promise me that you won't turn this into a shootout."

"We can do that." Jason agreed. "Is your rifle loaded again, Michaela?" He then nervously added, "Just in case, I mean."

"Yes."

"Then let's go."

With his arm feeling somewhat better now, Jason slowly opened the truck's door and crawled out, careful not to make any excess noise to alert Shade or his men. Michaela followed at his heels, and she silently shut the door.

Jason held his rifle in front of him and said, "Stay behind me, stay low, and stay silent." He pointed toward the campfire. "Let's go."

He began to walk away, but Michaela said, "No, come here."

Jason turned around and walked toward her. "What is it?"

She threw her arms around Jason, and the small girl stood on her tiptoes. Their lips brushed in a kiss. Once she broke away, she said, "Sorry. That was just in case."

"Nothing is going to happen." Jason consoled. "We have to stay positive. C'mon."

Moving low and silently, they advanced toward the camp. There was no movement or sounds coming from ahead apart from the enormous blaze of the campfire. Michaela whispered, "Are they still here?"

Jason peered through the darkness, looking toward the supply trucks. All of the remaining trucks were gone. He then turned to the makeshift helicopter pad and saw that the helicopter that had been fixed with the dusting equipment was gone as well. Speaking with a normal voice and standing straight up, he announced, "They left. They took the supply trucks and one of the helicopters with the cure."

"Shoot, we were too late," said Michaela. She paused and sniffed. "What is that awful smell?"

Jason looked around. "I'm not sure." He suddenly noticed a repulsive odor too. The smell of burning meat was wafting through the air. "We should check it out."

They advanced toward the camp, but Jason stopped in his tracks when he identified the source of the smell. Michaela noticed it too, and she said, "Let's go back to the truck."

"That sounds like a good idea."

They turned and slowly made their way back to the truck where Holder waited, leaving the camp grounds and the blazing campfire behind them, but not able to force the image of what they had seen out of their mind. The campfire was ablaze, scorching the bodies of the men and women Shade had killed—bodies of Jason and Michaela's friends. On top of the pile had been the enormous body of Teddy, completely consumed in flame. The image was nauseating.

Upon reaching the truck, Jason opened the door and said, "They are gone."

"I figured." Holder sighed.

Michaela asked, "So what do we do?"

"Well, I think there is only one choice." Holder pointed out of the front windshield. "There is the plane that we took from Australia, but I have absolutely no idea how to fly it, so we are stuck here until Australia sends more help."

"Oh, I remember them talking about that in the meeting. There are other airplanes in the colony."

"Yes. There are five more. And like Gordon had said, they will send help in a month if nobody comes back from the mission." He looked at the large plane looming in the distance before them. "But we can't just stay here for a month and wait for help while Shade and his men start raising a small army of cured creepers."

"We are going to follow them to Miami?" Jason started the truck again and turned on the headlights, which cut through the darkness.

"I don't know what else to do. We have got to stop Shade before he can go through with his plans." Holder opened the glove box and took out a roadmap. "We can follow this to get to Miami."

Despite the situation, Jason chuckled. "This isn't the first time I've done that." He began driving forward slowly. "Do we even have enough fuel to make it?"

Holder nodded. "It's about an eight-hour drive from here, but each of these supply trucks has a large reserve fuel tank in the back, so we will be okay." He then looked at the map. "Keep driving straight, Jason. We are going to be on this highway for a while."

The truck gained speed. Michaela asked, "So what is our plan? Do we try to catch up with Shade and his convoy and stop them from getting to Miami, or do we intercept them once they are there?"

After briefly pondering the situation, Holder said, "We still need to try to cure Drake, right?"

"That's the only reason I'm here." Jason admitted.

"Either Shade or one of his men is flying the helicopter to Miami, and the helicopter is the only way we can cure the creepers. If we attacked the convoy, there is a chance something might happen to the helicopter, and that is something that we cannot risk."

"Okay, so you are saying that we are going to take out Shade and his men but go through with the mission by ourselves? Is that even possible?"

"I don't see any other good choice," answered Holder. "But I do know how to fly a helicopter. If we can find it after we take care of Shade, then I can administer the cure, and we can stay in Miami and help establish the colony while we wait for help to arrive."

They drove in silence for a few minutes, thinking about the enormous task at hand. The mission had gone so wrong in such a short period of time, but Shade's plans had also failed because of their survival. After a few minutes, Michaela asked, "How are we going to kill Shade and his men when we get there?"

Holder answered with, "We will see how I am feeling when we get there. If I am able to walk, then we should all go and scope out the situation to come up with a plan after we know where Shade's base is set up."

Jason shot the idea down. "You were shot in the leg, Holder. There is no way that you are walking around Miami with us. I don't want anything to happen to you, and if we get into a fight with Shade and his men, then you won't be able to keep up. They will kill you for sure."

Michaela chimed in, "Yes, you have got to trust us. You are in no condition to help fight Shade."

With a sigh, Holder acknowledged. "I guess you are once again correct, but I didn't want to ask you two to take on such a daunting task on your own. The world is kind of resting on your shoulders." He thought about what he said and added, "I'm not trying to add any pressure."

Jason managed to force a laugh. "No, it's okay. I have to get my brother back right after Shade is dead."

Holder added, "As soon as we kill Shade, we have to find the helicopter so nothing happens to it. Can you do that, Jason?"

"I certainly can." He smiled. "That won't be too big of a deal. I'm sure they will land the helicopter somewhere fairly obvious."

"We will also need to set up some kind of base for the people to come to once they have been cured. We will hand out supplies and provide them with clothes," Holder said. "Let's just relax for a little while now, though. I learned in training that stress before a mission decreases chance of success."

"That's a good point."

"Thanks." Holder rubbed his leg again and said, "We will come up with a plan when we arrive in Miami, but we need to get there first." He turned on the truck's light again and consulted the road map. "I think I know how to find it. I have driven this part before."

The cabin became quiet and still, and the truck continued forward in silence. There was a long drive ahead and a dangerous mission at the end, but nevertheless the three people were trying to be positive, and in times like this, a good attitude seemed to be the only thing that could help them beat the impossible odds.

14

The noonday sun perched high in the sky above the third runway of the Miami International Airport. The airport was still and silent, apart from the sole truck driving alongside the runway. The truck had been unloaded of its supplies by Shade and then refueled before being driven to the large airport. It eventually came to a stop, and the driver got out—the large black figure of Truman. He leaned against the truck and waited, checking his watch.

Nothing happened. He climbed back in his truck and sat down for almost half an hour. He ate a snack bar and checked his watch again. After another ten minutes, he got out of the truck, and this time, he spotted what he had been looking for. A distant plane soared through the sky, and it was coming in for a landing. "About time," he muttered.

Truman searched the cabin of the truck until he found the signal flare he had stashed in the floorboard. He took it and detonated it, sending a bright red flare into the sky over the airport. After the flare went off, the plane seemed to change directions slightly, and after another few minutes, it looped around the airport and began coming in for a landing. Truman watched the plane, which was slightly smaller than the one the rescue mission had used, as its wheels engaged and reached down toward the ground. They made contact on the far side of the runway, and the plane thundered toward him. It progressively slowed and eventually came to a complete stop.

Truman smirked and jokingly clapped as the stairs descended from the plane. He leaned on the truck and watched several men—all dressed in combat pants and long-sleeved muscle shirts—climb down the stairs and begin unloading bags. He counted all seventeen that he had been expecting, including the pilot, and once they had all gathered their bags and weapons, he announced, "Welcome to America!"

One of the men, tall with long, dark hair, stepped forward. "Where is Shade?"

Truman pointed in the distance. "We found a hotel that we sat up for a base after we scared the creepers off. There are a ton of those things in this city, but then again, that was kind of the point. I'm glad you all have weapons."

The same man, who seemed to be the leader of the group of newcomers, asked, "How long until we start administering the cure?"

Checking his watch, Truman responded with, "About four and a half hours."

"Good."

"How did things go in Australia?" Truman's eyes scanned the line of buildings behind him.

The man answered, "Everything was fantastic. We snuck out and stole the plane at two in the morning. Almost everyone was asleep, but if any one actually saw us leaving, they still had absolutely no idea where we were going."

Truman couldn't help but smile. "That's great. They have no idea what is going on, and soon this city is ours for the taking."

"How have things gone for you? Did everything go according to plan?" The man spoke very bluntly with a monotone voice.

Truman dropped his gaze. "Well, there were, um, *complications.*"

"What do you mean?" The man looked Truman in the face and said, "Wait, somebody lived, didn't they? Somebody got away during the midnight massacre. Who was it?"

"Holder and the teenagers," mumbled Truman.

At this, the man laughed. "And you are worried about them? Two kids and a washed-up military man? It's three against twenty-five. I like our odds."

"Actually, we lost two men."

"Don't worry about them. There is no way our plans will be ruined, because we have worked too hard." He looked at the anxious faces of the other men. "Can we get going? We still have things to do."

"You're right, we better go." Truman walked to the truck and climbed inside. "I will drive slowly. Follow me on foot and be on the lookout for creepers. Like I said, they are everywhere." With that, he slammed the door, started the engine, and began leading the

CREEPERS 2

party of men out of the airport. They drove away slowly, winding through the airport and back into the city of Miami, the group of men walking briskly behind the truck. None of them noticed either of the two teenagers hiding nearby.

From behind a cement barricade behind where the truck had been parked, Jason and Michaela had been listening intently to everything that was said. They had been scouting nearby and snuck into the airport when they had seen the signal flares shoot into the sky.

Finally able to speak without risking being overheard, Jason said, "I can't believe there are more of them."

"From the sounds of things, they came from Australia." Michaela noted. "And they stole a plane."

"Yeah, that is bad. They are all armed, and the two of us can't kill them all." Jason shook his head and habitually checked his rifle to ensure that it was loaded. In the distance, the truck and the large group of men were disappearing around a building.

Michaela brought up another point. "Truman said that the mission was going to start in four and a half hours. We better hurry and get back to Holder so we can come up with some kind of a plan."

Jason shook his head at this. "We parked at least forty-five minutes away, and by the time we find the hotel they are using as a base, we won't have any time."

"What are you saying, Jase?"

"We can't go back to Holder. We have to take matters into our own hands." Jason stood up from behind the barricade. "We need to chase after them and see where they are going and come up with something on our own." He turned to Michaela, who had an uncertain look on her face. "We can do this. Think about everything that we have accomplished on our own. Come on." He reached out his hand and grabbed her by the arm, saying, "Let's go."

Michaela forced a smile. "You're right. I just hope Holder doesn't worry and come looking for us."

"We just have to hope that he won't do anything like that. But if we fail, it's honestly not going to matter what he does. If we die, then he dies too."

Jokingly poking him in the side, Michaela teased. "Way to think optimistically." Her actions helped lighten the mood. "Lead the way." She pointed the barrel of her assault rifle in the direction that the convoy had traveled.

"All right." Jason began slowly walking in the direction she had pointed. She followed him closely as he reminded her. "You heard what they said. We have got to be on the lookout for creepers." He didn't say what they both were thinking: any given creeper they encountered could be Drake. "Don't shoot unless you have to."

With this, they preceded forward, jogging after the convoy at a safe distance so they would not be seen. At the slow pace, it took several more minutes to make it out if the airport. Once they did, however, their pace increased while winding through the city streets. Memories came flooding back of their short stay in Miami. The city reminded Jason of how happy and secure they had been—him, Michaela, and Drake—when they had reached the settlement and been welcomed into the society. The thoughts of how fast everything had changed made him sad, so he pushed them out of his head and continued forward, refusing to dwell in the past.

The teenagers lingered about a hundred yards behind the convoy, moving low and silently so as not to attract attention. They were traveling down a street lined with tall buildings and plenty of abandoned cars, so finding places to hide was not too difficult. Ahead of them, the convoy turned to the right, down another side road. It disappeared from sight. That wasn't too big of a problem until Michaela grabbed Jason by the arm and forced him to stop in his tracks. She pulled him across the street, and they dove for cover behind a small blue car.

He looked at her. "What's wrong?"

She held her finger to her lips and then pointed to her ear. Jason stopped talking and listened intently. He heard a noise and immediately knew the source. From an alley ahead of them, the sound of predatorial growling came rolling out. He glanced at his girlfriend, and they both tightened their grip on their assault rifles. He whispered, "Creepers."

Michaela nodded slightly, trying not to attract the monsters' attention. Jason crouched by her, listening to the growls and trying to determine how many creepers were nearby. He decided there was either two or three, but it was hard to tell exactly. Judging by the sounds, they were only thirty yards away at the most. The growling was replaced by a snarl and then a long and drawn-out sniff of the air.

The teenagers shared a nervous glance. The creepers were coming their way, getting closer with every heavy step. Jason leaned down and peered under the car to locate them. He saw three pair of pale feet with long and filthy toenails. The beasts would spot the humans in mere seconds, which meant that there would be no choice but to kill them.

Jason gestured to Michaela to tell her to be ready with her rifle. She understood and put her finger on the trigger. She was tense but ready to spring up and attack in an instant. The creepers were just about to round the car. The sounds of heavy breathing and hungry snarls were frighteningly close.

Suddenly, they stopped. The creepers all froze in place and then backed up. Seconds later, they sprinted away down the street in the same direction that the convoy had traveled.

Michaela grinned at the bit of luck and said, "They must have heard Shade's men!"

Jason stood and began walking down the trash-covered street again before saying, "We didn't kill them, but Shade's men probably will. I just pray that none of them were Drake."

"That's a good point." Michaela sounded sad again. "So let's follow them and see where they went. The convoy still has to be close."

She was correct. After walking down the street and turning right, Jason and Michaela found the hotel that Truman had described as the base of operation only fifty yards away. Four large, dark trucks were hastily parked in front of it, including the truck that Truman had been driving to lead the men. The trucks had been unloaded, and the crates of supplies were stacked up against the building. None of the men were outside.

Michaela said, "No shots were fired, so the men must have been inside before the creepers arrived here. That's good news."

"Yes, it is, assuming the creepers decided not to hang around." Jason scanned over the building with his eyes and then said, "The penthouse windows are open, so I bet the men are meeting on the top floor."

"Do we just climb up there and fight them all? Try to take them by surprise?" Michaela sounded very skeptical. She added, "At least they are all in the same place."

"I'm not sure what else we could do." Jason was already walking toward the building. He asked, "How much ammunition do you have? Is it enough?" Michaela was about to answer, but Jason interrupted. "Wait! You answered our problem without meaning too."

She looked quizzical. "What did I say?"

"They are all in the same place!" Jason was already setting to work. He ran over to the stack of supplies from the trucks and began digging through them, obviously looking for something. First, he grabbed a syringe bagged in plastic that he found in one of the crates. "What is this?" He studied the covered syringe, which was filled with a clear liquid. There was a label on the plastic wrap, and he read it and concluded. "This is one of the cures that Shade injected into us at Gordon's house. I might as well hang onto it, just in case…" He was too nervous to even finish his wishful thought. He put the syringe in his pocket and continued searching.

"What are you looking for?" Michaela walked over to the crate and watched Jason vigorously digging through the miscellaneous items inside. She nervously glanced up at the hotel. "If we are going to go attack them, then we need to hurry before they come down."

Jason finally spotted what he had been looking for and exclaimed, "Here it is! Remember what Teddy told us? He said the crates were full of these." He held up a yellow cigarette lighter with a grin.

"What is that for?"

Beside the supply crates were red gas cans that had served as the emergency fuel for the supply trucks. He grabbed one of the heavy five-gallon cans and instructed. "Get one and follow me. We are going to burn this place down while they are still in it." With that, he lugged the can to the front entrance of the hotel, opened it quietly, and snuck inside.

Michaela, still standing outside, sized up the large fuel can and mumbled, "This is actually a great idea." She struggled to pick up the can, but then followed Jason into the dark lobby of the abandoned hotel. Upon entering the room, she found that he was already emptying out his fuel tank, pouring it on everything in sight. He soaked a couch, the carpet, the check-in desk, and then began heading to the stairwell.

By now, the entire lobby was overcome with the smell of gasoline wafting through the room. The putrid fumes made their eyes sting and water, but still Jason continued spreading the fuel throughout the entire lobby. He finally emptied the can and quietly set it down. He then took Michaela's can and said, "Get out of here. The fumes are too strong."

She shook her head. "You know I'm not going anywhere without you."

Jason, knowing that she wouldn't budge, reluctantly agreed. "Then follow me." He lugged the fuel can up the stairs, soaking them on the way. By the time they reached the second floor, the can was only halfway full. He proceeded to empty the fuel down the hallway and then said, "Let's get out of here."

They ran down the stairwell again, lungs stinging from the fumes. Jason looked around the lobby for a few seconds to admire his work and then said, "All right, we should go." They headed outside, but on the way to the exit, Jason took an old phone book from behind the admissions desk. After the brief stop, the two teens left the building, and both took a deep breath of fresh air.

"Good work." Jason praised. He took the cigarette lighter from his pocket and lit it and then danced the flame across the telephone book. He held the heavy book for long enough that it had been overcome with a blaze of flames, and then he looked to Michaela. "Here goes nothing." He threw the flaming book into the lobby of the hotel building and waited impatiently for the desired effect.

Whoosh. In mere seconds, the lobby burst into a complete inferno. A wave of intense heat rolled out the door and over Michaela and Jason. He couldn't help but laugh. "I hope they have fun getting out of there."

"So what do we do now?"

He pointed to the trucks parked a few yards from the building and said, "Let's go hide behind one of them just to watch and make sure Shade and his men don't somehow escape." He looked back at the blazing building. Flames were visible through the windows of the second floor. "When they smell smoke, they will come down to check things out."

They both walked away from the building, which was beginning to make popping and crackling sounds from the blistering heat inside. Jason knelt down behind one of the trucks, and Michaela sat beside him. She asked him, "What do you think Holder is doing? I know he was expecting us by now."

"He's probably really worried." Jason admitted. "But he would be proud of this, I think." He looked back at the blaze of the hotel building. The ground shook as a small part of the wall fell down, completely devoured by the fire. "I think everything is under control."

Suddenly, yelling became audible from the building. "The whole second floor is on fire!"

There was a crashing sound that was accompanied by human screams, and another voice said, "We've got to get out of here."

Jason swore and looked at Michaela. "I guess I spoke too soon."

"Let's kill them all. We can shoot them as they come out of the entrance—assuming they even make it out." Michaela stood to a crouched position and trained her rifle on the exit of the building.

"This is unbelievable," Jason muttered.

"What?" More screams came from the building.

"The creepers took out almost the entire population of the world, and we spent years fighting them, but the creepers aren't even the villains in any of this. What it all boils down to is that in a time of trouble like this, man's worst enemy is other men."

15

Both Jason and Michaela had killed dozens of creepers over the years, but killing a fellow human being was a completely different feeling. As the first three men, two of which had shirts that were ablaze from the fire, exited the burning building, Jason hesitated before pulling the trigger. He considered the weight that each shot carried and how any bullet could end a human life. He had to tell himself that they were bad men and that they would pull the trigger if he didn't do it first.

When he finally brought himself to do it, the rifle issued a spray of bullets into the crowd of three men. Over the years, he had practiced his way to deadly accuracy, and every single one of the seven bullets was placed well enough that it would have been deadly on its own. All three men instantly dropped to the ground in a large heap of bodies, blood, and flames.

Two more came out of the building, and Michaela took them both out with four bullets. Jason peered through the hotel's open entrance into the tall flames. Deep inside the blaze, the silhouettes of men were visible. One man collapsed to the ground, another was pinned under a large section of ceiling that caved in from the floor above.

Inside, one of the men yelled, "Where is Shade? Shade, are you in here?"

Another man replied, "He and Truman said they were going to the roof!"

Another part of the ceiling caved in, and a cloud of ash and smoke rolled out of the bottom floor. Jason looked to Michaela. "Why on earth would Shade and Truman go to the roof? This building is going to collapse in just a few minutes!"

"That makes no sense to me." Michaela looked to the top of the building. "Are they suicidal? There is no way to jump from up there and live."

Suddenly, Jason swore and stood up. "I'm going in there."

Michaela latched onto his arm. "What? Are you insane?"

Jason was talking fast. "The only reason they would go to the roof is if they had a way off." Michaela still stared into his face blankly, so he blurted out, "The helicopter is on the roof!"

"Oh." The weight of his words sank in. Michaela fell silent.

"If I don't do anything, then one of two things will happen: either Shade escapes or something happens to the helicopter. If something happens to the helicopter, there is no way that we can cure the creepers, and my brother dies."

"What are you going to do when you get to the roof?" Completely unexpectedly, a tear rolled out of Michaela's right eye, and Jason felt guilty. "I can't lose you," she said. "And if you go in there, I'm ninety-nine percent sure I won't ever see you again."

"I have got to do it though. This is the only way that there is a chance we win." He looked into her eyes.

"You aren't even sure that the helicopter is on the roof! You are just guessing." She blinked back more tears, and for the first time since Jason had met Michaela, she looked afraid. "If you're wrong, then you're dead for sure. Dead."

With another forced laugh, he said, "You don't have to remind me." The flame-ridden building made an ominous moan from behind them as if to emphasize Michaela's point.

"Well, do you know how to fly a helicopter if you actually get to it?"

Jason quickly responded, "My dad was a helicopter pilot, remember? I used to ride with him a lot when I was little, so I hope that I can remember enough to figure it out." Another long creaking sound came from the building, and he said, "I need to go, Michaela. I gotta be brave."

"Aren't you scared?"

Jason answered back, "Being brave isn't being fearless. It is acting even though you are afraid." He turned toward the building and then promised. "I'll be back, Michaela."

She weakly replied, "You better be," as she watched Jason disappear into the blazing inferno of a building.

Upon entering the hotel, Jason quickly glanced around to gather his bearings. To his right were the flames that were leaping up from the couch and dancing across the roof. At his feet was the ash of the phonebook that had started this entire thing. The majority of the ceiling had caved in and created a lot of rubble and debris in the lobby. The entire first floor was alive with flickering flames.

After peering through the smoke, he began making his way to the stairwell but made a point to stay away from the flames so that his clothing wouldn't catch on fire. As he progressed closer to the stairs and could see further into the smoke, he noticed a dilemma—one of the fallen roof sections was completely blocking his way to the stairs. He mumbled, "How am I supposed to get up there?"

Jason looked around the flaming room for a way to get to the second floor. A crackling sound came from overhead, and he leapt back as a large support beam crashed down exactly where he had been standing. A wave of sparks and ash blew toward him, and he turned away from them, feeling them sear the back of his shirt and jeans. He yelled out in pain, but whirled back around to face the beam that had almost crushed him. It was about twenty-five feet long, and one end had broken loose from the ceiling and fell to the first floor. It was flaming and unstable, but Jason knew that this might be his only way to get off the lobby floor.

Taking a deep breath, he stepped onto the slanting beam and began to slowly navigate it, shuffling his feet as he advanced. The smoldering wooden beam let out a creak from beneath his feet, and he said, "Please don't break." He harnessed his rifle so he could wave his arms to the side for balance and stability, which helped him climb up faster. The end of the beam that was still attached to the second floor caught on fire and began to blacken very quickly. The beam let out another groan under his weight, but he was only feet away from the top by now, so with two quick steps, he jumped onto the second floor. The beam crashed down, and flames erupted through the hole he had climbed through.

Jason bent down, hands on knees, to catch his breath and to try to get temporary relief from the relentless smoke. The heat was unimaginable and overbearing, but he knew that his only choice was to keep going forward. He stood and tried to peer through the thick smoke. He was in a hallway, and the stairwell was on the other end. As he watched, pieces of the floor were caving in between him and the stairs. Every second he wasted trying to recover took away from his chances of survival, so Jason decided he had to act now or never.

Taking no more time to stall, he began to run through the hallway. He leapt over the first gaping hole in the floor and felt flames lick at his ankles. The pain was blinding, but he continued forward nonetheless, landing on solid floor and looking at what lay ahead of him. There was no floor for almost the next twelve feet down the hall, for it had collapsed. A support beam was running perpendicular to his feet about halfway down the hole, and knowing not what else he could do, he took a measured leap and landed on the four-inch beam. He fought for his balance on the beam, regained it, and then leapt to the solid floor in front of him.

For a split-second, Jason thought he was safe. The stairwell was only feet away, and he was on what felt like solid floor. He felt a rumble beneath his feet, however, and had to sprint forward as the floor beneath him began to crumble away. Every step sent more of it caving in, but Jason miraculously reached the stairwell. He turned around to look at the hallway from which he had just came and shook his head in disbelief when he saw that the entire floor had completely collapsed, leaving only flaming walls and doors behind.

He coughed and continued up the stairs, stopping to look down the third floor hallway, which was also consumed by flames. At the end of the hallway, Jason counted six of Shade's men standing by a window. They shot the window several times, and it shattered completely.

One of the men yelled, "Let's go! We have got to get out of here!" He jumped out, and Jason imagined the man plummeting to the ground far below. The same man, who had obviously survived the fall, yelled back, "Come on! The fall isn't that bad." After hearing the words, the rest of the men jumped out of the window.

Jason was worried about Michaela. "I hope she can take care of them," he panted, still fighting for air. Taking a deep breath and focusing on the task at hand, he climbed higher up the stairs. He found that the fire had only made its way up about half of the building, and getting to the fresh air at the top of the stairs was a huge relief. He kept climbing, coughing the entire way, until he finally reached the door that opened up onto the roof.

Jason took a deep breath and said, "I can do this. I got this." He stepped back from the door again, worried by what he knew he had to do. His brother's fate, and potentially the world's fate, was resting on his shoulders. He dug deep inside himself and desperately searched for determination. He unharnessed his rifle and then said, "Here goes nothing."

For the first time, Jason felt the entire building shudder. There was no going back. With a powerful push, he threw the door open and ran out onto the roof.

Michaela watched six men, one by one, drop out of a window from the third floor of the building. They landed heavily and let out pained groans as they hit the ground from the great height. One man did not even manage to land on his feet. He lost his balance and fell to the ground, getting up slowly.

Michaela ducked behind the truck again and checked to make sure her rifle was loaded and ready. It was, so she moved in position to take fire. Pieces of the building began to fall to the ground. Smoke was pouring out of the bottom half of the hotel, and she was trying not to think about Jason being in it. The building was a flaming coffin for anybody inside.

The six men had recovered from the fall and dusted themselves off. The odds were certainly against her, but Michaela wanted to act while she could still surprise them. She braced to open fire and began to take aim, but suddenly one of the men yelled, "Get down!"

The men dropped to the ground as soon as Michaela pulled the trigger. The spray of bullets slammed into the building behind them as they rolled to cover behind another one of the trucks. She swore, knowing that she had lost the only advantage that she'd had on her side.

One of the men took charge of his group, yelling out commands to the others. There was a moment of silence from them. Michaela stayed hidden behind the truck, trying to think up a way to get out of the situation alive. She considered trying to run out of firing range, but reconsidered after deciding that she would certainly be gunned down by one of the six men.

"Fire!" The shout came, and then all six men opened fire toward the truck she was hiding behind. Bullets riddled the steel frame and shattered all of the windows. "This is so unfair." She returned fire blindly in the direction that the shots were coming from, but the blind fire did no good. Suddenly, all of the gunfire ceased, and the sound of men walking toward her seemed to scream out from the silence. The men's combat boots made their steps louder, and Michaela could tell that she was being surrounded.

"I surrender," she yelled. "You win! Don't shoot." The only reply from the men was their continued advance toward her. Seconds later, they walked around both ends of the truck, three on each side, with their rifles trained on her. She dropped her gun and threw her hands into the air, exclaiming, "Please!" She looked up into the eyes of the man who seemed to be leading the attack, pleading for her life.

The man shook his head. "We were instructed not to take any prisoner's alive. That includes you, sweetheart." He paused and aimed his rifle at the teenage girl. "Kill her, men."

Looking down the barrel of the rifle, Michaela took a deep breath. Her life was about to end, and she had survived so much to be killed by fellow human beings, which made the entire situation seem even worse.

The men were about to open fire on the girl when there was a thunderous cracking sound from the burning hotel. One of the outside walls on an upper floor began crumbling. Small pieces of debris showered down, and the men retreated a few steps backward, covering their heads. Suddenly, an enormous section of wall fell outward and hurdled toward the ground. One of the men looked skyward and noticed the slab of building thundering down toward his group, and he yelled out, but it was too late. Michaela saw it too, so she grabbed her rifle and jumped to her feet. She dove out of the way as the large piece of the building, still in flames, slammed down, completely crushing two of the trucks and five of the six men. A plume of dirt and ash burst into the sky. Michaela once again stood and whirled around. She raised her rifle and sent several rounds of bullets into the last of Shade's men, killing him immediately.

"It's about time I finally catch a break!" She looked at the truck that had been completely flattened by the large section of wall and then looked up at the burning building, surprised that it was still somehow standing. "You better be alive in there," she said as she ran her eyes up and down the burning building. Deep down, she knew that she was never going to see Jason again.

From somewhere behind her, Michaela heard a snarl above the crackling of the burning flames. She spun around with her rifle raised to identify the source of the noise. Her eyes locked onto a creeper that was fifty yards away but approaching her at a sprint. Her pointer finger instinctively reached for the trigger of her rifle.

Another large segment of the hotel wall fell outward, and she had to leap out of its way. The tremor the large piece of the building sent through the ground was powerful, she stumbled and dropped her rifle. The creeper continued its charge. Weaponless, Michaela was worried that the creeper was going to get to her before she could regain her rifle. Luckily for her, however, the beast abruptly stopped and cocked its head to the side as if listening for something. From somewhere above them, the sound of gunshots rang out above the sound of the flames. Michaela stood up and scooped her rifle from the ground before the creeper resumed its charge. She was ready this time and pulled the trigger on the dangerously close creeper.

Two bullets were all that it took to down the monster. They both penetrated its torso, and the creeper let out an ear-piercing scream as it dropped to the ground. A roar escaped its dying throat as it rolled toward Michaela across the filthy street. Its body bounced on the street and slid to her feet. The beast stopped in an awkward position on its back with its clawed hands clutching the bullet holes in its body.

Michaela stared down at the monster that had been attacking her. It had pale skin like all of the creepers, along with the bulging muscles and yellow eyes that, too, were expected. The beast's mouth opened to reveal fangs just like all the others of its kind. It convulsed and coughed up a thick glob of blood. But despite all of the characteristics it shared with other creepers, Michaela couldn't help but notice something unusual about the creeper. Its mutant face, even with the yellow eyes and sharp fangs, was recognizable. She had seen it before somewhere.

As Michaela stared down at the beast, her stomach began to sink, and she felt sick as she figured out what she had done. The beast was staring up at her with glossy eyes, but eyes that she recognized. This was Drake, Jason's brother, and she had shot him. She yelled out, "You're Drake!" His eyes slowly slid shut, and his head fell back into a small pool of blood.

Overcome with grief, she held her hands to her eyes and began sobbing. Her small frame heaved up and down as she cried. She collapsed beside the creeper and buried her face into her knees. Jason was certainly dead by now, and she had killed his brother, too. She sobbed for what seemed like days, and she couldn't seem to stop. The only thing that brought her from the stream of tears was a familiar voice.

"You have got to stop crying."

She looked up to see Holder limping up to examine Drake. He slowly kneeled down and put his fingers to the mutant boy's neck and announced, "He's not dead, and we might be able to help him."

She managed to get out, "How could we do that?"

Holder examined the bullet holes and said, "If we can introduce him to the cure, then we might be able to save him." He looked up. "It's not over yet."

Michaela tried to speak, but she couldn't make her mouth form the words. She felt as if there was an enormous rock in her throat.

Holder forced a desperate smile. "Don't give up hope. He can be saved as long as we can get to the helicopter soon. Where is it?"

Completely hopeless, Michaela once again buried her face in her knees, and the sobbing continued.

16

As Jason burst onto the roof, his eyes stung from the combination of smoke and bright natural light. He coughed again and surveyed his surroundings. The roof was open and flat. On the far side of it, the helicopter was roaring to life, just as Jason had anticipated. Truman sat in the pilot's seat, and another figure was walking briskly toward the chopper.

Jason yelled out across the roof, "Shade!"

The brilliant man turned around, and a look of recognition flickered across his face. He was dressed in combat clothing with an ammo belt slung over his shoulder like the rest of his men. "So you were the arsonist responsible for all of this." He smiled and turned completely around to face Jason. "I'm impressed that you found me."

"I've always been one to impress." Jason held his rifle up and aimed it at Shade.

"Don't waste your time, Jason. You don't want to get into a fight with me." He took a pistol from his belt and confidently grasped it, looking at Jason.

"You want to turn this into a gunfight, Shade?" The building beneath their feet quaked.

"No, but I can't let you ruin my plans." Shade looked around the roof at the smoke that was rising and the few flames that were visible at the building's edges. "I'm creating a new world! It's going to be a beautiful thing, unlike the aristocracy of Australia that I escaped."

Jason was sickened. "So it's true. That's why you did all of this, because you want to create a new colony?"

Shade nodded. "You are smarter than you look." He stepped backward two paces toward the helicopter and elaborated. "I was tired of not being appreciated like I should have been. I was not given enough respect."

"You were number two in charge, right behind the minister!" Jason advanced toward the man slowly.

"You are exactly right, I was number *two*! I was taking orders from Gordon, but he knew nothing about leading people. I am three times the intellectual that he is, but he rarely used my opinion and treated me like a dog. I was only given my position because he was afraid of making an enemy of me." Shade reached up to his ammo belt and grabbed something. "But now isn't the time to talk about all of this. I better go. I have a new country to create after all."

Shade held up the object he'd taken from his belt. Jason recognized the shiny black sphere as a hand grenade. He watched the pin drop to the roof and yelled out, "Don't do it!"

Nevertheless, Shade tossed the grenade toward Jason. It bounced twice and rolled to the boy's feet. He swore and sprinted away as the small explosive detonated and blew a hole in the hotel's roof. Jason dove to his knees to avoid shrapnel, and he lost hold of his rifle in the process. He cried out as his weapon skidded over the edge of the roof and plummeted out of sight.

Shade made a break for the helicopter, laughing as he went. He still had the pistol in one hand, but it dangled lazily at his side. Diving on the roof had aggravated the cut in Jason's arm and tore two of the stitches loose, but nevertheless, he pushed himself up and turned to face Shade. The man hadn't even noticed Jason was on his feet, so this was the perfect opportunity.

Jason sprinted forward, around the hole in the roof, and charged at Shade from behind. Shade heard him approaching and whirled around. He held up the pistol and aimed it hurriedly at Jason's chest. The boy expected this and was prepared, ducking just as Shade pulled the trigger. The bullet sailed overhead. Shade swore and aimed his gun again, but he wasn't quick enough. Jason lowered his shoulder and slammed into the man, knocking him off of his feet, and both of them tumbled to the roof. The pistol slipped out of Shade's hand and skidded away. When they smashed into the roof, Jason was on top of Shade looking down on him with hatred.

From inside the cockpit, Truman yelled out, "C'mon, Shade! Get up."

In response to the outburst, Jason balled his fist and punched Shade with all of his strength. The blow landed in the center of the man's face, and Jason felt Shade's nose break under the force of his punch. Shade's head was slammed back into the roof, and he grabbed at his nose as blood began to rapidly pour out and his eyes began to water profusely. The man swore and kicked at Jason, knocking him off. Shade madly looked around him and located his pistol about ten feet away on the roof. He struggled to crawl toward the weapon, but Jason regained his composure and latched onto Shade's ankle. He stood and pulled the man backward.

"I refuse to let you ruin things. You can't mess this up," Shade yelled up at Jason. He jerked his ankle out of Jason's grasp and rolled away before leaping to his feet. Around them, more smoke was billowing up, and it was obvious that the fire was getting closer to the roof. In the center of it all stood two men, staring at each other with determined expressions and raised fists. Both of them had their body weight on the balls of their feet to allow for quick reaction. They were equally drenched in sweat and ash from the heat and intensity of the fight.

Neither of them spoke, but instead only glared at each other. Jason considered attacking first, but he could tell by the look on Shade's face that he was getting anxious. He was right. Shade lashed out with his fist sailing toward Jason's head, but the boy ducked the blow and retaliated with a strike of his own that dug into Shade's shoulder. Next, Jason kicked out and pounded his heel into Shade's ribcage. The attack was so powerful that Shade was thrown from his feet and rolled toward the edge of the roof.

He stopped near the edge and looked up at Jason. His broken nose was still bleeding profusely, and he was wheezing, clutching his side where Jason had kicked him. "You ruined this, you ruined everything." He winced in pain and stopped talking for a minute. "And I think you broke my rib." He rubbed his side delicately.

"Well, maybe you shouldn't have killed all of the campers. They were good people, but you just used them like pieces of a game. You turned them into pawns and discarded them when you were through." Jason stepped forward. He was now looming over the broken man.

Suddenly, the building groaned again under their feet. It shook violently, but remained standing. Jason looked back to Shade and was surprised to see tears streaming down the man's face. He sobbed out, "I don't want to die here. All I wanted was a better colony, more power, and the respect I deserved." He looked up to Jason. "I'm not a bad man!"

"You certainly convinced me otherwise when you killed Teddy and all of the other campers that were willing to risk their lives on your behalf. You even tried to kill us." Jason shook his head as Shade continued sobbing at his feet.

"Please, Jason! I'll change. Give me this chance." He glanced across the roof and then wiped blood from his face. "Help me get to the helicopter. I am not armed, and you can get in the chopper first. We will cure the city together, and you will get your brother back." His eyes pleaded up at Jason. "You can see Drake again, and helping me is your only chance." The building quaked again under their feet. Shade looked up pleadingly, outstretching his hand to Jason. "Please, Jason, help me."

Jason didn't budge. He asked, "How do I know that I can trust you?"

"I'm not in a position to fight back."

He shook his head. "That's not good enough for me, Shade."

Shade wiped more blood from his face and pointed to the pistol he had dropped. "Get my pistol! Kill me if I try anything."

Jason stepped backward and did as Shade had instructed, picking up the pistol. He made sure it was ready to fire, just in case, and then pointed it at the man lying near the edge of the roof. "Get up."

Shade nodded and rolled to his side slowly. He reluctantly took his hand off of his broken rib and tried to push himself up, but he let out a cry of pain and fell back to the roof. "I can't do it."

"Try again." Jason waved the pistol at Shade. "Hurry. We don't have much time."

The hotel let out a shriek and shook. The fire had almost devoured it completely. From inside the helicopter, Truman's deep voice thundered out, "We've got to go! This entire building is about to fall." The blades of the helicopter were spinning furiously, ready to take off at a second's notice.

Shade tried to push himself to his feet. From on his side, he got his hip about six inches off the roof, but then he shouted out in pain and fell back again, clutching his side. He turned toward Jason. "Help me!" He sounded completely desperate as he outstretched his hand up to the boy.

On the far side of the roof, a loud noise roared above the crackling of the flames. Jason whirled around to look and gasped at what he saw: a large part of the roof had crumbled away, and huge flames were reaching up through the gaping hole. Jason swore and looked back at Shade. "All right, let's go."

Pistol in his left hand, Jason leaned down and grabbed onto Shade's hand. Shade groaned out as Jason began pulling him to his feet. He said, "Thank you so much. Holder was right, you really are a hero. I know it took a lot to be able to forgive someone who was as cruel as me." He gave Jason a weak smile.

"I think there is good inside every man," Jason replied. "Just like I think that deep down there is good in every creeper, too."

"You are such an admirable young person." Shade acknowledged. "And that is why I almost feel bad about doing this." Still holding onto Jason's hand, Shade pulled violently with unexpected strength and threw Jason forward. He stripped the pistol from the teenaged boy's hand and watched as Jason lost his balance and fell over the edge of the roof. Jason began plummeting downward but managed to twist around and grab onto the roof's ledge with both hands.

Jason screamed out at Shade, "You lied to me!"

"Of course, I did! You are too trusting, just like Gordon. Trust can be a downfall, you know." Shade smiled sinisterly as he aimed the pistol at Jason's face. "And it looks like the tables have turned, my friend. I hope your brother will be less of a nuisance than you were." He stepped on Jason's left hand, crunching the fingers underneath his boot. Jason yelled and let go of the roof with his hand, now only having four fingers of grip.

Jason looked down. The ground was so far away. Flames still poured out of nearly all of the windows, and some were high enough in the building that they were licking at his ankles, which he pulled up out of their reach. He managed to say, "I hate you."

At this, Shade laughed. "Well, I'm not too fond of you either. My new colony won't have any people like you. I'm going to build the perfect place. I'm going to turn the United States into a Utopian society. If people oppose me, then they will be harshly punished."

"You are a sick man." Jason felt his fingers slipping and knew he couldn't hold on for much longer.

"I'm not completely horrible, Jason. I'm going to show you that I can be nice."

Feeling the building shudder again, Jason said, "Well, you better hurry."

Truman yelled out, "Just kill him already, Shade. We've got to go!"

"The human body has two hundred and six bones in it," recited Shade. "And if I were to let you fall, you would feel the vast majority of those bones break, and your skeletal structure would be obliterated. Your organs would be punctured, and you would die an unimaginably painful death."

"Then help me up," Jason retorted.

"No." Shade raised the pistol. "I'm going to shoot you and save you the pain. One bullet between your eyes and you will never feel pain again."

"Go to hell."

"One day, perhaps, but not yet."

Jason watched Shade's finger reach around the trigger. The pistol's barrel was a gaping black hole of death staring him in the face. Shade's finger tensed.

Suddenly, the loudest noise Jason had ever heard in his life thundered out. The building shook so violently that he knew he was going to be thrown from the ledge, but he managed to hold on. There was an ear-piercing sound, and the roof under Shade's feet began crumbing in. A look of absolute horror stretched across the man's face—wide eyes and an open mouth—and he screamed out. Shade flailed his arms, trying to grab hold of something, but to no avail. In a mere instant, he plummeted into the inferno of the building, and flames burst up from the hole to greet him. His screams lasted for several seconds before suddenly ceasing.

Jason couldn't believe the sudden good luck. He reached up and grabbed onto the ledge with the hand that had been stepped on. He then used his feet to push against the side of the hotel and fought to pull himself up onto the ledge. When he made it back on top of the building, he looked down the gaping hole that had consumed Shade. All across the building, the roof was beginning to cave in. He scanned through the smoke in search of the helicopter which he located about twenty yards to his right. Truman was still staring back with a look of absolute shock on his face after witnessing Shade's death. He seemed to be in some sort of a trance.

Acting quickly, Jason began to sprint for the helicopter. It was obvious that there was hardly any time before the building collapsed. In the cockpit, Truman seemed to snap out of his trance. He began flipping switches, and the helicopter blades spun even faster, preparing for takeoff.

CREEPERS 2

The building shook one last time. This time, however, was unlike the others. It felt different—more complete. As the boy continued sprinting across the roof, the entire building began a slow collapse. Large sections of the roof were caving in, and Jason had a sensation of falling. He still continued forward, nevertheless, refusing to completely give up hope.

Ahead of him, the helicopter lifted off. It became completely airborne and began rising while the rest of the building surrounding it continued the steady fall. A large hole crumbled away only feet ahead of Jason, and he leapt over it. Flames lapped at him through the hole, but he continued forward. There was no other choice. Every footfall was unstable, and any step could be his last.

Still, the helicopter was only feet ahead now, rising higher into the sky. Jason looked up at the landing skid, the long metal rod attached to the bottom of the chopper, and prayed he could reach it. It seemed so far above his head.

He coiled down on the disintegrating roof. Every muscle in his body tensed and prepared for the fateful leap. Time seemed to slow. All around him the building was disappearing. He was encompassed by a circle of flames. Smoke suffocated him and stung his eyes. The intensity of the heat was too much to comprehend. With one last breath, he sprang upward, rocketing into the air and reaching up for the chopper. His arms reached out farther than he thought possible, straining to stretch to the max. The landing skid was only inches away, and Jason yelled from effort.

The relief was overwhelming when the hot metal of the skid struck both of his palms. He grabbed on in a steely grip as the helicopter rose into the sky. Turning his head, he saw the hotel building completely collapse in an enormous ball of flame that rocketed three hundred feet into the air and let off a wave of heat that washed over the chopper. As he hung from the bottom of the helicopter, Jason knew he was far from safe. He was losing his grip, and the ground was sinking farther and farther away, but he couldn't help but smile. Shade was dead and gone, but the helicopter and, therefore, the cure, had survived.

He looked up at the long metal cylinder that was welded to the side of the helicopter above him. The lives of so many creepers depended on it. He was beginning to have a little hope until Truman's voice called out from above, "You have ruined too much. It's time that you finally die, Jason."

Then the gunfire began.

17

Michaela looked from the mutated body of Drake to the pile of ashes that had been the hotel only half an hour earlier. Together she and Holder had moved Drake away from the building before it had collapsed, but he was still bleeding from the wounds she had inflicted.

Holder was inspecting the wounded creeper and trying to figure out what could be done to save him. Michaela managed to fight back tears long enough to ask, "Is there anything that we can do for him?"

Holder bit his lip. "I really don't think that there is. If the helicopter has been lost, then there is nothing to do but stay here with him and be there as he passes." He looked at Drake's pale fanged face. His breathing was barely detectable now. His clawed hands were clutching at the wounds through the tattered remains of a T-shirt.

Michaela cried aloud. "I can't believe this. I lost Jason, and I lost Drake." She felt nauseous and dizzy.

Suddenly, Holder stood up and looked into the sky. "What was that?

Michaela wiped her eyes. "What?"

Suddenly, she heard the noise too. The sound of gunshots rang out from within the billow of smoke in the sky. She counted five shots, all coming in a row before Holder once again asked, "What is that?" He pointed to the smoke as something began to emerge out of it. A whirling sound was becoming increasingly louder, and Michaela couldn't believe her eyes as the helicopter emerged from within the smoke. Even more amazing was that a teenage boy was visible hanging from the bottom of the chopper. Holder gasped. "What the…"

"That's Jason!" Michaela cut him off.

Holder only shook his head. "That boy can survive anything, I swear." He looked to Michaela. "If anybody can survive this, it's him."

Michaela couldn't tear her eyes from the helicopter and her boyfriend dangling beneath it. "Please hold on, Jason." She begged. She soon realized that slipping was not Jason's biggest problem, however. The girl gasped in horror as she realized from where the sound of the gunshots was coming.

Jason cursed as Truman threw up the emergency switch of the helicopter's door and opened it enough to lean out and take fire. He had a nine-millimeter pistol and shot several times, but Jason managed to dodge the fire by swinging back and forth on the landing skid. The downward torrent of air caused by the spinning blades was intense, and Jason struggled to hear anything above the sound, but he managed to make out Truman saying, "Just stay still!"

Jason refused to obey, and he used his hands to shuffle along the skid until he was near the back of the helicopter and out of range. Truman pushed the door open even more and leaned out so he could take better aim, and once again he sent four more bullets soaring past the boy. Jason breathed a sigh of relief as they all missed him, but he knew that with any amount of time, his luck would end unless he took action.

Truman ducked back inside the cockpit to pilot the helicopter and temporarily left Jason dangling underneath the helicopter on his own. "How can I get out of here?" He looked above him. The helicopter was very large with two doors on each side. On this side, the front door was for the pilot, and the back door was for passengers. Jason considered trying to climb up the landing skid and enter the helicopter from the back door, but he realized that would be impossible because when Maxwell had welded the duster to the helicopter, he had welded it over the back door so that it would no longer open. "Are you kidding me?" He was losing strength, and he was straining to hold on.

The ground was at least three hundred and fifty feet below, and Jason felt his stomach lurch when he looked down. He was running out of both time and hope when he had his next idea. On the far side of the helicopter, the other side of the landing skid hung down. He sized up the distance and decided that the other side was about six feet away. Attempting to swing to the skid would almost certainly mean death, but it seemed to be Jason's only chance because Truman would be back to kill him at any second.

Jason closed his eyes and thought back to before the virus and the apocalypse. He thought back to when he was in the first grade when he would go out to the playground with his friends. They would spend every recess swinging back and forth on the monkey bars. He had wasted many afternoons like that during school. When he opened his eyes again, he visualized himself back on the monkey bars surrounded by a group of his old school friends, all of whom were now long dead. With his hands growing tired, he began to swing on the skid, kicking his feet back and forth and using his momentum to sway his body. He kept the movement up until he was swinging farther forward each time. The time was right, and he knew that if he waited any longer before acting, then he would talk himself out of making the leap, so with a deep breath and the opportune swing, Jason let go of the skid.

Being completely airborne was the most terrifying moment of Jason's life. The ground was a dizzying distance below, and he held his breath for the split second he was soaring through the air. He had a hold of nothing, and time seemed to freeze as he soared to the skid on the other side of the chopper. Falling to the ground would be the most horrible and painful death imaginable, but he forced the thought out of his mind and reached out. Jason grabbed the skid ahead of him and breathed a sigh of relief as he tightened his grip on it. Using his hands, he turned around so that he was

CREEPERS 2

once again facing the chopper and smiled as he heard Truman open the pilot's door again and, no longer seeing Jason, say, "Well, I guess he finally fell off." Jason once again had the surprise factor.

Still, his hands were growing even more tired, and he knew he could not hold on for much longer. He kicked his feet up and wrapped his legs around the landing skid. He held on with a tight grip and pulled himself around so that he was lying on top of the skid as opposed to hanging underneath it. The temporary relief made his tired and sore hands feel a little better, but he could not continue to rest for much longer. Looking at his surroundings, Jason was not sure where Truman was flying the helicopter, but one thing was certain: he had changed his plans and was heading out of Miami instead of dropping the cure.

"I've got to stop him." Jason looked up and saw both of the helicopter's doors looming above him. On this side, however, the back door was not welded shut. "If I could get in back there, then I could attack Truman from behind." He knew that Truman was armed but figured that if he could enter in the back of the chopper, he would be slightly more protected than if he entered the front. Even with the element of surprise, the odds were still against him.

Jason pushed his torso up from the skid and reached up to grab the handle of the rear door. He pulled it, but nothing happened. "It's locked." The door was made of tinted glass, and through it, Jason could see an emergency handle that would unlock the door from the inside. He leaned back down on the skid and debated about what he should do. The ground seemed even farther below now, and it was clear that the helicopter would not be landing anytime soon. There was only one thing he could do.

Sitting up, Jason carefully balanced on the landing skid. He calmed himself and focused on the window, which was a challenge, considering the distracting blades that whirled around above the chopper. He mentally pictured what had to be done, reared his fist back, and then struck the glass window.

It did not break. A spider web of cracks danced across the thickly tinted glass, but it refused to shatter. Jason pulled back his throbbing fist and let out a whimper from the pain. With his legs still wrapped around the landing skid, he rubbed the hand that he had smashed into the window. He felt like he had done just as much damage to the hand as the thick glass. Still determined to put a stop to Truman's plans, Jason balled his other hand into a fist. He once again reared back and used almost every muscle in his body to deliver another focused strike. This time, however, the window completely shattered, and Jason reached his entire arm into the helicopter. He pulled the emergency switch down and threw the door open, sending wind rushing into the cabin.

Truman whirled around and yelled out, "How on earth…?" He saw Jason peering into the helicopter and immediately understood what the boy had done. "You are unbelievable."

Jason, knowing that he was shielded from direct fire, briefly took his eyes off Truman as he was climbing into the backseat. When he looked back up, Truman's pistol stared him right in the face.

Bang! Jason dove into the backseat just before a bullet blazed through the air where he had just been. It soared out the helicopter's open door. Truman screamed in frustration and brought the gun back to fire again, but the boy was too fast. He snatched the pistol and ripped it from Truman's grasp, now pointing the weapon at him and demanding, "Land the helicopter."

Truman turned away from Jason and the gun for just long enough to study where he was flying. He spoke slowly but loudly enough to be heard above the roaring propellers and the rush of wind into the cabin from the open door. "You are very resourceful and talented, Jason. I will give you that."

Never taking the pistol off of the man, Jason closed the back door of the chopper, and the noise died down substantially. "Bring the helicopter down, or I will kill you."

Truman shook his head. "No, you won't. I'm not an idiot, Jason." Truman pointed to the complex control board that was used for flying the plane. "Do you know what any of these controls do?" There was a pause. "I didn't think so." He punched a couple buttons and threw a switch on the panel. "If you shoot me, then we both die. To make matters even worse, you lose the precious cure that your brother's life depends on."

"You can't say that!" Jason was yelling.

"I'm not the one with the zombie brother." The large man turned and stared coldly into Jason's eyes. "If you are really going to shoot me, then do it now. Don't just stand there and waste your breath with a bunch of pointless threats. Do it." He sneered. "Be a man of your word."

Jason was extremely tempted to pull the trigger, but for some reason he could not make himself do it. "Land the helicopter or die."

"It looks like I'm going to die because this bird isn't going down." Truman seemed too confident, like he knew something that Jason did not know.

Jason kept the pistol trained on Truman. "No, do it now!"

Truman shook his head. "I'm sorry, Jason, but I have something else I'd rather do."

The man moved at very impressive speed, acting in an instant. He snatched a bag from the seat beside him, heaved the pilot's door open, and threw himself out of the helicopter. While beginning the freefall, he strapped the bag to his back, and Jason realized that it was a parachute. As the pilotless helicopter lurched forward, he mumbled, "Oh, you've got to be kidding me."

Pistol still in hand, the boy hurriedly climbed from the backseat to the control panel and looked at the buttons, switches, and foot pedals. Deciding what his priority was at the moment, he leaned out the open door and located the parachute cutting through the air about a hundred feet below. The chopper was beginning to fly unsteadily and out of control, but Jason used one hand to hold onto the door frame, and with the other, he leaned out and took aim with the pistol. He clutched it tightly and fired a dozen times. All of the bullets hit their target, tearing sizable holes in the parachute. Truman screamed as he started falling faster. The parachute was doing him no good at all after Jason had punctured it. The boy couldn't help but smile as he watched Truman plummet to earth.

Crawling back into the cockpit and closing the door, Jason studied the control board. He thought back to the times he had spent flying a helicopter with his father, but he had been very young and had forgotten much of what he had learned. Still, some of the basic controls looked familiar, and Jason began to experiment with them. The helicopter was swiftly diving to the ground below, but by throwing two levers up, he stabilized it.

Then came another big dilemma. "How do I turn this thing?" He located something that resembled a joystick on the control board and said, "Maybe this is it." He pushed the joystick to the right, and the helicopter turned to the left. "Oh, it's inverted." By pulling the stick toward him, the helicopter lowered in altitude. "Sweet."

After understanding the basic controls, Jason was faced with a big decision. He looked out the window beside him and saw the metal cylinder welded to the side of the helicopter. The question now was what should he do: try to drop the cure over the city, or land the helicopter so that Holder could do it? Both answers seemed to have positives, but his biggest concern was that if something were to go wrong while landing the helicopter, he could wreck, and the cure would be lost for good, and dropping the cure while he was flying would ensure that didn't happen. Still, he realized that he could run out of fuel and that he wasn't sure which of the gauges would show him how much he had left.

"I better land this thing and let Holder do it. He's the experienced pilot." With the decision made, Jason grabbed the joystick and turned around the helicopter. He scanned the horizon and located the billow of smoke coming from the ashes of the former hotel building. He knew that this is where he'd left Michaela and that she would be worried sick about him, so he flew in that direction.

On the streets below, creepers were very active. They were all heading to the smoking hotel. From within the cockpit, Jason watched some of them while wondering which one was his brother. The chopper continued forward and flew closer to the hotel. Jason began sizing up where he wanted to land.

Soon he was flying over the hotel but not brave enough to try to land on the confined space of a street. He scanned below for his girlfriend but could not locate her, so he continued forward. The white sand of the Miami beach glowed some four hundred yards ahead of him. Jason decided that the beach was the perfect place to land the chopper. It was this very beach that the Australian journey had begun when Holder had saved them from the swarm of creepers months ago.

Five minutes later, the helicopter was flying above the beach, and Jason was trying to figure out how to stop it. He read a few buttons on the control board and then threw a switch. He was fortunately right, and the chopper began hovering in place. He pushed another button, and the rotary atop the helicopter began slowing down, and the chopper began descending slowly. He sat impatiently in the cockpit and waited.

Two minutes later, the landing skid from which he had been hanging only minutes earlier touched down in the sands of the beach. He turned the engine off, and the propellers began to slow.

"Thank you, God." Jason looked to the sky and breathed the biggest sigh of relief that he ever had in his life. He was safe now, the cure had survived, Shade was dead, and for once in his life, everything seemed to be going his way. "I've got to find Michaela and Holder."

He opened the helicopter's door and jumped down to the sandy beach, facing the ocean. Waves rolled up to the beach and came near Jason's charred and blackened shoes. He took just a moment to look at himself in the reflection of the water. His face was blackened with soot, and his clothes were charred. "I look horrible." Chuckling at this, Jason brushed his hair back out of his eyes.

"Jason!" He heard Michaela's call from across the beach, but something was wrong. She wasn't happy. Instead, she seemed terrified.

He whirled around and began to run back to the city. "Michaela! Where are you?" He spotted her emerging onto the beach, and after looking closer, he noticed that Holder was limping beside her. He was worried. "What's wrong?" As he got even closer, he could tell that they were carrying the limp body of a creeper. He began to recognize the features of the wounded and blood-soaked beast and mumbled, "No." Tears began rushing down his face, "No…no…no…no…" Michaela and Holder laid the limp body of Drake down in the sand. "No!"

Jason was running at a full sprint and bawling at the same time. He ran up to the body of his brother and collapsed in the sand, tears streaming down his face. Michaela knelt beside him and threw her arms around him, sobbing as well. She managed to say, "Jason, I'm so sorry." She tried to say more but burst back into tears.

Holder forced out, "He is alive but barely. We wanted you to have time to say goodbye" He knelt down in the sand beside the teenagers.

The only thing Jason could say was, "Is there anything that we can do?"

Holder looked to the helicopter. "If we could get the cure into him, then we might be able to save him, but that's not even a guarantee." He paused. "I'd guess he only has minutes left, and there is no time to fire it up and use the cure." Holder put his hand on Jason's shoulder. "I'm so sorry."

"So that's it? We just watch him die after all of this?" Jason couldn't fight back the tears that were streaming down his face.

"I had one other idea." Holder admitted. "But unfortunately, I wasn't fast enough." He gave Jason time to respond, but the boy was crying too hard. "Each of the supply crates from the trucks had a medical kit in it, and each of the kits had an emergency cure antidote inside. I was going to get one, but the building collapsed on all of the supplies."

A spark of hope ignited in Jason's mind. He stood up and dug into his pocket, struggling to form words. "Just a second," he said. His heart sank when he felt nothing, but then he searched inside the other pocket, and his hand wrapped around what he was searching for. He took out the syringe that he had taken from one of the medical kits outside the hotel and shakily handed it to Holder. "Is this what you are talking about?"

A look of astonishment flickered across the man's face. "How did you get this? Where did you…"

"I'll explain later." Jason interrupted. "Just use it!" He looked down at his dying brother, looking past his fangs and clouded yellow eyes to what was deep inside—the brother he so dearly loved. Drake had very nearly stopped breathing.

Holder ripped the syringe from the plastic wrap and stared up at Jason. "I can't promise that this will work, but it is better than nothing." He stabbed the syringe into Drake's chest and emptied the contents. "Say a prayer."

The three stared down at their dying friend.

18

"Thank you, sir."

"Not a problem." Jason nodded at the middle-aged woman as she took the bundle of clothing from him and began walking away. From where he was leaning against the table of clothing, he could not help but grin as he looked around at all the people walking to the beach, many of whom were familiar faces from his short stay at the Miami settlement. One thing was for absolute certain: the cure had not only worked, but it had worked exceptionally well. Holder had landed the helicopter about two hours ago, and cured creepers were already emerging from the city to the small camp that had been set up on the beach.

"Where should I put this basket?" He turned around and was greeted by the completely human version of his brother, who was limping around and assisting in any ways that he could, although he was moving much more slowly than usual.

"Um, put it under that table." Jason pointed to the sand, and Drake did as told.

Drake laughed and said, "I know that I've said this a lot, but I'm so glad to be back."

"I couldn't agree more."

Jason knew that he would never be able to explain what had happened and how the cure had fixed his brother—for that matter, he doubted even a doctor could—but the change had been breathtaking. As soon as Holder had emptied the cure into Drake, it almost instantly began to work. Drake's breathing had improved, and within five minutes, some of the color began to return to his pale skin. The calcium that had built up on his teeth to form fangs crumbled away in tiny particulates that looked like dust. As the cure coursed through Drake's bloodstream, Jason and his friends had watched in absolute amazement as the bullet holes in the boy's flesh began to slow the bleeding before their eyes. Nobody could explain what had happened, especially since Shade was dead, but when transforming back into a human, Drake's gunshot wounds were also being healed. A few hours later, he had regained consciousness, sitting up and opening his eyes to reveal a welcomed blue color. By that evening, Drake had fully changed from a mutant preparing to die to a teenaged boy on the mend.

Michaela's voice snapped Jason back from his moment of recollection. "Look at how many of them there are, guys."

The brothers looked up to see another twenty people emerging from between the city buildings. They all looked confused while scratching their heads and talking to each other. Holder, who was walking around the table beside Drake, yelled to them, "Come this way, folks! We have clothes and food! We can help you."

After Drake had been healed, they had spent the rest of the night going into the city and gathering clothes and food in baskets and loading them into the bed of the truck they had taken to Miami. After several hours and truckloads, Holder decided that they should have enough supplies to accommodate the people, so they set up the clothes and food on tables they had taken to the beach. Holder had dropped the cure, and ever since then the four were working at the table, giving both supplies and explanations to the confused-yet-healthy humans who had come from the city.

As the group came even closer, one of the men in the front asked, "What happened, and how did we all get here?" He gestured around to the humans in tattered clothing, "And why are we dressed like this?"

Holder explained what had happened, how the entire city had been transformed into creepers and how the colony in Australia had come up with a cure. He only left out the part about Shade and his men attempting to overthrow the Australian minister and start a new colony in the United States. While he explained, Michaela and the brothers made sure that every newcomer had new clothing and food.

The group's original plan was to bring tents to the beach and set them up for the cured humans, but Drake had suggested another idea. He and Jason had explored a large hotel sitting adjacent to the beach and in clear sight from the primitive camp. They found it to be fairly undisturbed, and the cured humans were invited to stay inside, at least, temporarily until they had recovered and knew where they would go next. So far the plan was working, and Jason estimated that around eighty people had already journeyed to the hotel as a refuge.

"This is amazing." Michaela tugged on Jason's arm. He turned to face her, and she rose up on her toes and kissed him. "Look at how many people we have helped!"

"I know. We are so lucky to have gotten to be part of it."

Drake, who had been filled in on everything that had happened leading up to his curing, wisecracked, "Yeah, Jason, it sounds like you *really* are lucky to be part of this. Can you tell me the part where you were hanging from a helicopter again?"

"I will later." Jason smiled and considered what his brother had said. He thought about the dangerous things he had done and somehow survived: climbing through a burning building, fighting Shade on the roof, jumping on the helicopter. There had been so many instances that if things had not gone exactly as he had hoped, then he would be dead.

More people came to the table, and Jason and his group continued catering to them. They kept this up for another few hours, and it was very rewarding. They witnessed tears of joy as family members were reunited, and they met many people who praised them for what they had done. Additionally, they had also met many interesting people. One man named Isaac said that he had been an electrician and that he would try to find a generator that he could use to power the hotel.

One of the biggest surprises of all came from a familiar face. As the sun was beginning to hide behind the horizon, a recognizable voice came from across the beach. "I knew you kids were special, and something told me that I would see you again."

Jason looked at Drake and then to Michaela. They all reached the same conclusion. "Redman."

They were correct. Soon the tall frame of Jeremiah Redman came walking up to the table of clothing. This man had been their first friend in the Miami settlement, and they had explored part of the city with him.

Jason shook Redman's hand. "It's nice to see you back." He introduced Redman to Holder, and the two began discussing the teenagers. Holder told Redman about Jason setting the hotel on fire and leaping onto the helicopter. Redman then shared similar stories from his time with them, and the two men showed that they had quickly struck a friendship. After talking for almost another hour, Redman said that he was going to go to the hotel, but that he was looking forward to talking to them the next day. He left, and the four saviors were left alone on the beach under the light of a full moon.

"I think that was probably all of them." Holder looked to the city. "How many people do you think that we cured?"

Jason shook his head. "I honestly have no idea."

"Hold on just a second." Drake got up and walked away, coming back seconds later with a pad of notes. He studied it in the moonlight, obviously counting, "We saw two hundred and thirty-seven people."

"I'm impressed," said Jason. "You actually took notes."

"Well, of course!" Drake nodded. "After my time as one of them, I just want to know how many others we helped who were like me. I feel connected to those people, for some reason."

"I can understand that," Holder said.

Michaela asked something that had, at some point, crossed all four of their minds. "So what is next? Where do we go from here?"

"That's a good question." Holder smiled. "But I think it is one we can answer." He looked up at the full moon hanging in the sky. He continued, "These people are in no condition to be left on their own. We don't have any way to get back to Australia."

Jason asked, "So then we stay?"

"Yes." Holder nodded. "Australia will send a rescue plane over here in less than a month since we will not have returned. They might even send one sooner because of Shade's men stealing one. That had to arouse some questions."

Drake seemed to really like the idea of staying. "That's great! We can stay here and help these people establish their own temporary colony."

"We can certainly do that. That was the original plan, after all." Holder grinned at the youngest Bennett brother's enthusiasm. "There are many skilled people that we have saved—an electrician, two carpenters, a former mayor—I'm sure that these people will be able to rally together and establish something like our colony back in Australia."

"This is a great opportunity to make a difference." Michaela acknowledged. "I understand why Shade wanted to be the one to save these people. They respect us so much. Shade could have had a small army in his complete control."

Holder stood up. "It's a good thing that we didn't let that happen." He looked across the dark beach. "If there are for sure no more people left to be cured, then we can go get some sleep. It's been over a day." He rubbed his eyes.

"I didn't even know how tired I was until I sat down here and stayed still for a little while." This came from Michaela, who yawned and leaned her head back into the chair she sat in.

"Well, don't get too comfortable yet." Jason teased as he hopped to his feet. "C'mon, Drake." The younger brother followed him down the beach, and together they began gathering large pieces of driftwood until both of them had large armfuls. They brought the dry wood back to the camp and threw it into a big pile. Jason further arranged the wood before taking the same lighter out that he had used to burn the hotel down. He lit the pile of wood and backed up as the flame grew to a raging campfire.

"Good idea," Holder said.

"Thanks." Jason glanced to the city one last time. "Just in case there are any more people in the city, we need this here, so maybe they will come to the beach and find clothes."

Drake asked, "So where are we camping? Should we go stay in the hotel with all the people that we saved?"

"As large of a hotel as that is, it has to be really full from everyone that we sent there." Holder ran his eyes up and down the dark building. Then he pointed to another building nearby and said, "I saw that store is called Outdoor Explorer. It looks like a bunch of camping and hiking gear, so I bet we could find some tents in there and set them up right here. That way we will be here if anybody sees our fire and comes looking for help."

"Good idea."

The tired group quickly walked across the littered beach to the store. They broke inside and found several tents, which they carried back near the fire and pitched in the sand.

Holder shook everybody's hand. "Great job today, guys. You have done so much, and I can't express what you mean to me." He kicked out his leg and laughed. "Even my gunshot wound is feeling better."

"You need to stay off it for the next few days. I'll find you some crutches around here somewhere." Jason gave the man a hug from the side and said, "We all owe you a thank-you as well. You have done so much for us, and you are the reason that I got my brother back."

Drake grinned. "And it's so good to be back. Being a creeper is arguably the worst thing that can happen to a person."

"*Arguably?*"

"You are hungry the entire time. It's hell."

"I have absolutely no doubts." Holder looked at his tent and then at the teenagers. "Now let's get some sleep. Tomorrow we start the recovery process."

No sooner had he spoken the words when from off in the distance came a shout, "Oh my gosh. It can't be…"

Three shadowy figures were emerging into sight on the beach. The three teenagers followed as Holder broke into a jog.

He quickened his pace in the direction of the words and barely managed to say, "There is no possible way…" After a moment, he added, "I can't believe my eyes… Tanya!"

As the teenagers watched, the figures came into sight: a blonde woman, a teenaged girl, and a young boy, the latter two looking just as confused as the teenagers felt. The woman instantly embraced Holder and began to cry. "James," she managed to get out. "I thought you were dead."

Holder was temporarily speechless, but finally he managed to say, "Boys, Michaela…this is my wife. This is Tanya."

Jason looked to his brother and Michaela, both of whom looked completely baffled.

Tanya spoke. "James, this is your son." She looked to the boy. "JR, meet your dad."

Holder knelt down beside the boy and gave him a hug as well. He looked like he was about to cry, but he said, "I always dreamed that you two were alive somewhere. JR, you have no idea how badly I have wanted to meet you, my son."

The boy hugged Holder back around the neck, saying, "Hi, Dad."

Holder looked to the third of the newcomers, the girl, and asked, "Who are you, sweetie?"

"My name is Anna," she responded. "I have heard so much about you, James."

The storybook reunion quickly turned into nearly an hour of recounting how Tanya's group had survived the virus and reached Miami and Holder and the teenager's side of the story. Holder was happier than the brother's had ever seen him now that his family had been reunited. Finally, after countless stories around the campfire, they decided to call it a night and put off the rest of the reunion until the next morning.

"Good night," Drake told everybody. "Being human is way more exhausting." He then looked to Anna, who seemed to already be bonding with the youngest Bennett brother. "I can't wait to talk to you more in the morning, Anna."

"I agree," she said. "It was so awesome meeting you." After a hesitation, she added, "And your friends."

Drake smiled, walked away, and disappeared into his tent.

Holder glanced at Jason and Michaela and said, "I'm going to take my family back to the shop to find a couple more tents and sleeping bags. You two need a moment." He began walking away but then turned back one last time. "Thank you…for everything." He disappeared into the night.

Anna had frozen in hesitation on the beach. She asked, "Do I get to go too?"

From out of sight, Holder chuckled and clarified. "When I said I'm taking my *family*, that definitely includes you. Come on, Anna. You are one of mine now."

With the beach suddenly to themselves, Jason looked to his girlfriend. "I'm so glad that we are both safe." He was completely taken by surprise when Michaela suddenly lashed out. She stomped her foot on Jason's shoe, and he yelped and jumped back. He exclaimed, "What was that for?"

"That was for having to watch you hang underneath a helicopter five hundred feet in the air." She paused. "Oh, and leaving me to run into a burning building." She looked up into his eyes. "Don't you ever do it again because next time the punishment will be so much worse."

"Oh, come here." Jason grabbed Michaela and pulled her against him tightly. She wrapped her arms around him, and he rested his chin on the top of her head. They hugged and rocked back and forth in the sand for a moment.

"Jason?"

"Yeah?"

"I…" He felt her look up at him, then returned her dark gaze. "I kinda… love you."

He grinned and hugged her even tighter as he ran a few fingers through her long hair. "I love you too." He really did. He rubbed her back as they stayed there in an embrace for what seemed like an eternity. She looked up at him again and kissed him, but this time it was more than just a slight brush of lips. There was strong emotion, and he could feel it.

"Um…guys? I'm right here." Drake's sarcastic tone was carried with the sound of the waves crashing.

"Oh…um…yeah," Michaela muttered as she stepped back, nervously smoothing her hair.

"Let's get some sleep. Tomorrow is going to be an important day." Jason gave her another quick kiss and made his way to his tent, crawling inside and lying down.

Only seconds later, Michaela's head popped through the entrance, and she said, "There's no way I'm letting you sleep in here alone."

"I'm totally okay with that." Jason smiled at her, and together they lay down on a blanket. There was silence for a moment until he said, "Thank you so much for what you did for me. I never would be here without you."

"I know." She wrapped her arm around him. "But just stop talking. I want one more kiss."

Their lips met one more time, and Jason realized he was happier than he had ever been. The virus had been defeated, his brother was back, Holder had been reunited with his family, and most importantly, they were all finally safe. After the kiss ended, he told her, "Goodnight, Michaela."

"Goodnight, Jason."

THE END

ACKNOWLEDGMENTS

I once again feel beyond humbled and blessed to see another book with my name on it. I truly hope you enjoyed the story of the *Creepers* series, and this book, just like the last, would be nothing without love and support from a multitude of people.

First of all, thanks to God for loving me and supporting me every step of the way. He has blessed me with all of my talents, and everything I do goes to His glory.

Next, thanks to my publisher, who once again helped birth the book I had envisioned from the start.

Thank you to both my parents, who guide me daily through this great big storm that we all know as life. You both are amazing, and that is why I dedicated the book to you. You were the first two to ever read this book (other than my first round of editing, of course), and I still remember Mom's blunt honesty when she said she didn't like a lot of it and that it needed to change. That being said, thanks to both of you for helping me with suggestions as to how I could improve it, and hopefully you both like it now!

I have had so many amazing, supportive teachers, but I will only name a few. Mrs. Irving came in clutch by teaching me science for three years in a row, and it was in her biology class that I began to concoct the idea for a cure. (I do realize it is a long shot, but this is sci-fi, okay?) Ms. Bardin was a huge help and somebody I could turn to regardless of what my problems were, writing or otherwise. Thanks for that. And Mr. Parker, my high school principal, was especially pivotal. He helped me build a web site (www.jessehaynesauthor.com) and gave me all the guidance I needed through my senior year in high school. Thank you so much, Mr. Parker. I hope we can stay friends for many, many years. Also, thanks to the wonderful professors I have had so far at the University of Tulsa. Professor Peters is already revolutionizing my world view, so expect something big for my next book. (Wishful thinking, at least.)

Once again, I have had some amazing friends throughout this process. I can't name them all, but I will definitely try to mention a few. To Coach Dillman, my fatherly figure, who proofread this book very early in the process, along with Ms. Kim Zehender, who caught the vast majority of my typo and logistical flaws. To Emily, who has always been such a supporter of my writing. To Grant and Tristan (T-Love), who have been endless bounties of inspiration; my friends whom I can turn to in any time of need; to Haylie June, who gives me the best, most sincere advice when I'm way too stressed out with "author stuff," as I call it. And even (wait for it…) to Sydney Herring, the super deep-thinking, beautifully poetic writer that I know is going to be a famous wordsmith one day. I'm calling this one right now, boys and girls.

Last, thank you to Ms. Darleen Bailey Beard, for providing me with countless opportunities and being extremely supportive.

Thank you for everyone who has offered me support throughout the book writing process, from the teachers who invited me to speak at their schools, to all the awesome students I have met along the way, to my fans who have supported me through this entire journey. From the bottom of my heart, thank you all. You are my inspiration and the reason I keep chasing this crazy dream.

Share this book with your friends (preferably not physically) and help spread #creepersnation.

May my stories continue bringing you an escape to adventure.

—Jesse Haynes